THE TRADE
EXPERIMENT

THE TRADE EXPERIMENT

THE CHINA AFFAIRS

BOOK 2

BRAD GOOD

CHAPTER 1

It was strange to feel like a celebrity, but that was exactly how Jack Gold felt now that he was back in China.

Davis had informed him on the private jet back to Beijing that Jack would not be staying at the Marriott; rather, Wang Yang had insisted Jack stay at a hotel closer to him, which turned out to be a high-end boutique hotel light years more decadent than the business-styled Marriott.

The hotel's manager, a man named Jim, had escorted him to an opulent suite with huge picture windows overlooking a garden and a pool. Jack had heard about these hotels before—there were hundreds of them throughout the country, meant for senior Party members, who had the best of everything, no expense spared. And Jack found this to be true, even in the shower, where the soap was *L'Occitane*, from Provence, in Southern France.

It had surprised him, though, when he went downstairs, freshly showered and in clean clothes, to find Jim the only other person in the hotel.

"The hotel was emptied for you, for this visit," Jim said. He gestured to his left. "And here is our cigar lounge."

Jack nodded at each amenity Jim pointed out, though he couldn't help but feel strange, being the sole occupant of this hotel.

"We have a chef on staff twenty-four hours a day, so any time you feel hungry, you can come down here or call for room service. Order whatever you'd like. It's an honor to have you as our guest."

"Thank you," Jack said. What he wanted right now, more than anything, were some eggs and hashbrowns. No matter how talented the chef employed here was, Jack was willing to bet he wouldn't be able to properly cook that American breakfast classic.

"If there's anything you need, just let us know. We want to make your stay here as comfortable as possible."

"I appreciate it."

Jim excused himself after that, leaving Jack to wonder what he was supposed to do now, alone in a hotel. An entire hotel, all to himself! Not necessarily a scenario he ever dreamed of being in, yet here he was. He wandered around, peeked into the cigar lounge, walked past the heated pool, his restlessness growing. He made his way toward the empty lobby, where two of his security detail agents were standing near the front door. Though they were only here because they had to work, seeing familiar faces helped a little in quelling the feeling that he was trapped in a cage.

"I wasn't expecting the entire place to be cleared out," Jack said.

Tom smiled. "Well, it certainly makes our job easier."

"Not a bad place to have all to yourself," Denis said.

Jack's phone beeped, and he eagerly pulled it out of his pocket, knowing it wasn't going to be Jojo, but hoping anyway. "Excuse me one moment."

It was Andrew San.

Hey *dàgē*! his message read. *How are you? WHERE are you? I couldn't believe my eyes when I saw you broadcast on TV!*

Jack sighed as he looked around the empty hotel. It'd be great to see Andrew, but it wasn't like he was about to hop on a train from Shanghai to come up here. *I was surprised to find myself on TV too. Maybe we can get together when I get back to Shanghai, in Beijing right now.*

Andrew's reply was instant. *Oh wow! Me too, what are the chances? Want to meet up for a drink?*

Jack was so pleased at the strange coincidence he didn't bother to think twice about it as he wrote back an enthusiastic Yes! Andrew suggested the Jianguo Hotel, and Jack was more than happy to be on his way.

"That was a friend of mine who would like to meet at the Jianguo Hotel," he told Tom and Denis.

It was close enough that he could walk, and a wave of relief washed over him as he stepped out of the hotel, Tom and Denis following a few yards behind.

As he approached the hotel, he recalled the last time he was here—when he met with the three men—Ari, Joshua, and Tony—who would accompany him to the Control Center. How were they doing? He'd have to try to get in touch with them soon.

But first—Andrew. Jack smiled at the sight of his friend strolling up, smoking. Andrew waved, took one last drag, then put the cigarette out.

"Dàgē!" he said. He eyed Tom and Denis for a moment, but then returned his attention to Jack. "I haven't been able to stop thinking about you since I saw your face on the news! What are the chances we'd both be in Beijing at the same time? I'm glad it all worked out! Let me buy you a drink."

They went inside and took a seat at the bar. After they ordered and had their beers in front of them, Andrew turned and looked at Jack. He didn't say anything, but instead spent several seconds just looking at him, until Jack finally smiled.

"What?" he said. "Do I have something on my face?"

"Your face," Andrew repeated, returning Jack's smile. "Jack, I almost didn't believe it at first when I saw you on TV. How long had you been planning that? Was that your intention all along? I thought you came to China for the excellent business opportunities."

It was hard to read Andrew's tone—he sounded a bit incredulous and perhaps a little in awe. But Jack had a feeling there was also a fair measure of disapproval there too, though his friend was doing a good job at keeping it in check.

"I did," Jack said. "And obviously, I can't get into all the details. It was just one of those situations that I ended up involved in. But not the reason why I came to China at all." He shook his head. "You know that."

"Do I?" Andrew raised his eyebrows. "I really couldn't believe it. There I was, just got home, cracking open a beer, wondering what I was going to do that evening, and wait a second, I recognize that voice on the TV. I was in the kitchen and the TV was on in the other room, I heard you before I saw you. But I *knew*, I just knew, that it was you, even before I went out there to look."

"It must've been a shock."

"*That's* putting it mildly! And then Stanley starts messaging me and wants to know if this is something I knew about. Can you believe that! As if I'd be part of something like this." He took a sip of his beer and shook his head.

"It's for the good of everyone," Jack said. "We did it because we wanted to improve things for everyday people here. They deserve it. They deserve to have the freedom to make their own choices based on uncensored, factual information. Don't you agree? Isn't that what you'd want for yourself?"

"Of course I want what's best for myself," Andrew said, grinning. The smile turned into a laugh. "Seriously, though, I hear what you're saying Jack. And I still think you're a good guy. I just didn't realize you were also a TV personality." He glanced over his shoulder and then back at Jack. "You do realize that you're something of a celebrity. You have your own security. Obviously you're now someone important. Have you noticed the way people are looking at you?"

"I'm trying not to," Jack said. "I don't like being recognized every time I go out in public." Yet it was certainly something he'd have to deal with now, he was realizing. Yes, people's attention spans seemed shorter these days, but what had just happened was a very big deal—the sort of thing that children would be reading about in history books decades from now.

"Seems like maybe you should have thought about that before you decided to get in front of that camera," Andrew said. He tapped the neck of his beer bottle with his index finger, frowning. Jack thought he sounded a little sad, or maybe disappointed that Jack would have decided to go such a route.

"Look," Jack said. "I know it was probably a big shock to see me on TV like that. Trust me—it wasn't my plan to be the one sitting there. And we did this because we truly believe that it's the best thing for the regular, everyday citizens of this country."

Andrew's eyebrows shot up. "Is that what you told yourself?"

"Of course," Jack said. "Because we believe it. People should have free access to information, to facts, whether or not they paint a particular leader or government in a rosy light. How are people supposed to think for themselves and make informed choices if they're only being given one side of the story?"

Andrew looked at him incredulously. "Because it's worked out so well in other parts of the world? In America? You Americans and your liberties—sure, it all *sounds* well and good, but your country is a mess. People shooting each other up in schools, at churches. Your healthcare system is a disaster. People only care about wealth. And themselves. Let's say something big happens, some sort of pandemic that requires people to put the good of the whole ahead of their own selfish wants and needs.

Citizens of China can do that. But Americans? Europeans?" Andrew shook his head. "That's the problem when you place more emphasis on individualism. It'll just screw you over in the end."

Jack regarded his friend, nicely dressed in an expensive-looking gray button-down shirt and a pair of designer jeans, black leather shoes. "People in America care about more than just wealth," he said, "though I won't argue that it is an important component of the American Dream. But it's not even wealth, really—it's the freedom to be able to live life on your own terms. And yes, for many that means cultivating a successful career and enjoying the liberties that money can afford."

"But this is China, not America," Andrew said. "How can one country claim to know what is in the best interest of another? America certainly has a penchant for that sort of thinking."

Jack took a sip of his beer. Out of the corner of his eye, he could see a couple seated at table nearby looking at him, then looking down at their phones, then back to him. They whispered to each other. He had a feeling that, at any moment, one or both would be lifting the phone to take his picture.

"I think I better get going," he said.

"But you haven't even finished that drink."

Jack picked up the bottle and drained the final sip. "I'm sorry I can't stay out longer. I'm sure you can understand that it feels a little strange to be back, especially considering some people actually recognize me."

"Of course they do. You're the most recognizable man in China right now. How come you're so surprised? Surely you knew that would happen."

Jack paid for their drinks, then patted Andrew on the shoulder. He wasn't going to be able to put it into words that Andrew understood— why he had done it, why he had risked so much for so many people he would never meet in person. "I'm glad we met up," he said. "Thanks for getting in touch. And we'll get together soon, and hang out for longer next time, I promise. Things are still settling down. They're not going to be like this forever."

"I guess you're right," Andrew said. "I just wish you had thought about things a little more before you went and did it."

"Maybe," Jack said, "but if I spent too much time thinking about it, I probably wouldn't have done anything. Action was needed in this situation, not endless pontification."

The expression on Andrew's face was hard to read. He just needed to wait and see how things were going to improve. The changes that would come for people because of it. Jack was certain his friend would eventually come to realize that the right thing had been done.

*   *   *

The next morning, for his meeting with Wang Yang, Jack chose a bright yellow tie to go with his navy-blue suit, and at eight-thirty exactly, he made his way downstairs. Davis was waiting in the lobby with Tom and Denis.

"Good morning," he said as they exited the hotel. "Our vehicles aren't allowed to enter the compound, so they'll take you in their car." He pointed to a dark gray Audi parked in front of their SUV. "But don't worry—we'll be nearby."

A few minutes after they started driving, Jack's black phone beeped. He pulled it out of his pocket and read the message: *Turn off this phone before you give it to them at Zhongnanhai.*

They were going to Zhongnanhai, the Communist Party's base? Most of the Politburo Standing Committee lived on the twenty-two-acre property, which had formerly been the imperial garden in the Imperial City, located next to the Forbidden City and closed to outsiders.

As they turned, Jack stared out the window and saw they were entering the Xinhuamen, the "Gate of New China." He could see two slogans on the side of the entrance; one read "Long live the great Communist Party of China" and the other said "Long live the invisible Mao Zedong Thought." He could not help but feel humbled by the history of this place, and at the same time in awe of the traditional Chinese architecture.

Once within the compound, they continued down a road toward the more modern-looking office buildings. The car slowed to a stop where a man and a woman waited for him near the entrance.

"Hello, Mr. Gold," the woman said as he approached. "We are here to guide you to your meeting." He followed them through one set of double doors, where he relinquished his phones to a gentleman who was waiting right inside. He continued on his way through an extensive set of corridors, passing by offices, some with their doors open, others closed. They went through a door and Jack found himself outside; to his right was a lake, and they walked along a path toward another building, which they entered, wove through more corridors, and then exited to the outside again. There was a pool house and an elegant pagoda, under which were two tables and several chairs, partially hidden by willow trees and bamboo.

Wang Yang sat at one of the tables, smoking, a stack of paperwork in front of him. He looked up as they approached, a broad smile on his face. He stood. "Hello, Mr. Gold," he said. "I'm so glad to see you so soon again."

"Likewise," Jack said. He smiled at his two guides, who had turned and were starting to walk back the direction they had just come. "Thank you," he said.

"Have a seat. Have a smoke." Wang Yang pushed the pack of cigarettes toward him as they sat down. "Would you like a drink?"

"I'll try any tea you recommend," Jack said as he pulled a cigarette from the pack.

An attendant appeared, and Jack lit his cigarette while Wang Yang told them what type of tea to bring out. Then, he took another cigarette from the pack and lit it, leaned back in his chair. "Jack, I just have to ask— do you know what you've done?"

Jack exhaled a plume of smoke. "To be honest, I haven't gone online much. I haven't even watched the news. So, yes, I know what I've done, but I haven't been paying much attention to what other people are saying about it."

Wang Yang nodded. "One of the things you said: *tiāngāohuángdìyuǎn.* Which literally means *heaven is high and the emperor is far away—there's no help for it.* When you said that, you got people's attention. Everyone knows that saying and believes it, but they never talk about it. You helped elevate the consciousness of a nation. You were humble and honest. You didn't try to hurt anyone. You were truly acting in the interest of others."

The attendant returned with a tray with their tea. "Oolong," Wang Yang said. Jack watched as he put some of the tea in the tea pot and then added the hot water. He swished the water around the pot several times and then poured it out. Because the tea leaves were handpicked and then left outside to dry, it was a custom in China to wash the tea before it was consumed to clean it and "wake up the tea." Wang Yang added new water to the pot and let it steep for a few moments before pouring a cup for Jack.

"I must ask," Wang Yang said, "how long did you practice that speech?"

Jack set his teacup down. "Let me first say I'll never speak to the Chinese people uninvited again. And, as you probably heard, I wasn't even supposed to be the person up there talking. Tony Woo was, and I'm sure he had something great prepared. I had a few minutes to prepare, but honestly, I think it was better that way."

Wang Yang regarded him. "A few minutes," he said slowly. "Incredible. But I think you're right—that's why it sounded from the heart. Not rehearsed."

"I truly love China." Jack paused. He hadn't been sure when and if he would bring this up, but now seemed as good a time as any. "And . . . more importantly . . . I'm in love with your daughter." Wang Yang nodded and took a drag off his cigarette. "She thinks I'm a spy," Jack continued. "Which I'm not. But she's very upset with me, and I do understand why. I want to make amends and to continue our relationship. I'd like nothing more than to marry her. If she agreed, would we have your blessing?" He was certainly putting the cart before the horse, but he had to ask, even if Jojo never spoke to him again. Perhaps she had said something to her father, something that Wang Yang might pass along to him now that would let Jack know if reconciliation was even possible.

"If Jojo wants to marry you, then yes, you have my blessing. But not for at least three months; things need to settle down."

"Of course," Jack said. "And if I know Jojo at all, *she'll* be the one who decides when she gets married."

"I do control when she gets married," Wang Yang said. "Here, the father has the Hukou Bar. You can't get married without that."

"That's true," Jack said. In China you had to go to the town where the bride's family is formally registered and use the family documents, called the "Hukou Bar" when getting married. "She could travel to the United States and get married there."

"That would be difficult without a passport," Wang Yang said. "China confiscates the passports of its leaders and their relatives. They can't travel unless approved."

Jack pulled Jojo's new US passport out of his pocket and slid it across the table. Wang Yang gave him a quizzical look before picking it up.

"I met with Sutton and asked him for it," Jack said. "And if Jojo is willing to give me a second chance, I'd like to ask her to take a brief trip with me to the US. If that's okay with you."

Wang Yang closed the passport and handed it back to Jack. "As we both know, Jojo's an independent person. And Chinese law says that if she has another passport, it's up to her whether she wants to travel. It's not my place to approve or not." He paused. "If you get married, will you promise to do so in China?"

"Only if you have better Maotai here than we can get in America," Jack said with a smile. *Maotaijiu*, an aromatic and very strong, clear alcohol, was China's national liquor. It was so renowned that Henry Kissinger had once said, "I think if we drink enough Maotai we can solve anything."

Perhaps, Jack thought, he should imbibe some of the stuff before trying to solve the issue of Jojo never wanting to see him again.

"Do you really like Maotai?" Wang Yang asked.

"I love it. It's just hard to find."

"Let's see what we can do about that." Wang Yang gestured for one of the attendants to come over, and he spoke to him in a Suzhou dialect. The attendant nodded several times and then disappeared.

Jack was considering whether or not to indulge in another cigarette when he saw a man approach. As he came closer, Jack thought he looked familiar. He wore tan slacks and a navy blue shirt, and he walked casually, not in a rush. Jack blinked. Was that . . .? No, it couldn't be . . .

But it was.

It was Zhao Lihong, and he was smiling.

Jack stood immediately, and the former president of China went right over to him, took Jack's hand in both of his, shook it warmly.

"I . . . I didn't mean to cause any difficulty for you . . ." Jack stammered. What was going on? Zhao Lihong was probably the last person he expected to see here.

"You did me a big favor," Zhao said. "No need to get into it all now, but let's just say I was being pressured to do things I would not normally do. I should be thanking *you*."

Zhao took a seat and helped himself to a cigarette, so Jack did the same.

"Jack's in love with my daughter," Wang Yang said, looking at Zhao. "Look what he got when he met with Sutton." He nodded to the passport, and Jack handed it over for Zhao to look at.

"I was in his office and he asked if I needed anything," Jack said, as Zhao flipped through the pages.

He gave an approving nod as he handed the passport back. "Can you get me one of these, too?"

The three men laughed. They had some more tea and finished their cigarettes, and then Wang Yang asked if they could take some pictures. Four photographers rushed out, as if they'd been waiting in the wings for this very moment. They stood with the lake in the background, their pictures being taken from every angle—first, the three of them, then just Jack and Wang Yang.

After they were done with pictures, the current president and the former president walked with Jack back the way he came. The man Jack had surrendered his phones to gave them back, and Jack said goodbye to Zhao Lihong.

"I'll walk you out to the car," Wang Yang said as they stepped outside. "What's next for you?"

"I have to go to Shanghai," Jack said. "See if Jojo will even talk to me. I guess it's going to be difficult to explain myself if she doesn't even want to see me."

"She's independent and stubborn," Wang Yang said, "but she is also compassionate and forgiving."

"I hope she'll be able to extend some of that forgiveness to me."

"You have the passport?"

Jack felt his pocket, even though he knew it was already there. "I do."

Wang Yang smiled. "Well, if the passport and your apologies don't work, try a dog."

"Huh?"

"A dog. Jojo's always loved animals, and recently she was talking about getting a dog. The topic comes up every few years, and she always decides that it's just not the right time. But when is it ever going to be the right time?"

Jack thought back to their very first date, the picnic they went on and the dog that had run over to visit. He wouldn't mind having a dog, and he certainly wouldn't mind having one with Jojo, but he wasn't sure if showing up on her doorstep with a dog would be the best way to begin making amends.

"Things will work out for you, Jack," Wang Yang said. He shook Jack's hand and then opened the car door. He gestured to a bag Jack did not recognize. "Two bottles of Maotai. Jojo likes that brand. Good luck."

"Thank you," Jack said. He slid into the backseat and shut the door. A passport, her favorite drink, and possibly a dog. He hoped that would be enough to win Jojo back, but there was only one way to find out.

CHAPTER 2

The Didi driver regarded Jack skeptically.

"He'll be fine," Jack said, glancing down at the black and white puppy in his arms. "He's very well behaved."

The driver frowned but then relented, and Jack and the Border Collie mix he had adopted from the Shanghai SPCA got into the backseat. Jack also had with him a bag with the two bottles of Maotai and some puppy food and dog toys. He had almost decided against the dog, but he figured he would have one shot at getting back with Jojo.

Not wanting to show up completely unannounced, he sent Jojo a quick WeChat message that he was going to stop by quickly. Unless he received a vehement NO, he would proceed with his plan to go over and talk with her in person.

Jack held the puppy in his arms when he knocked at Jojo's door, which was slightly ajar, probably to let the gentle breeze through. The puppy, who had spent the majority of the ride over asleep on Jack's lap, suddenly wriggled out of his arms and nosed its way inside. Jack opened his mouth to call the dog back but realized he didn't have anything to call it.

"Hey!" he hissed, not wanting to cross the threshold before Jojo had invited him in. "Come back here!"

He couldn't even see the puppy anymore, and he hoped that it wasn't sniffing out the perfect corner to relieve itself in. Before he could decide what the appropriate next move would be, he heard Jojo yelp in surprise.

"Oh! Where did you come from?"

"Hi, Jojo," Jack called, and he gave a sheepish wave as she came into view. She had on jeans and a white button-down shirt, the sleeves cuffed and pushed halfway up her arms. Her hair was up in a topknot and just the sight of her made Jack's heart leap. She had a smile on her face because she'd just been looking at the dog, but when she saw him, the expression vanished. "I sent you a message," Jack said, "that I was just going to stop by, I hope that's okay."

She took a few more steps toward him, but stopped far short of being close enough for physical contact. Arms folded across her chest, one eyebrow slightly raised.

"I got your message," she said. "I assumed it was to come over and tell me in person some tall tale about how you're not really a spy. I didn't realize it also included meeting your new dog. I didn't even know you had a dog. But—" And now a smile did cross her face, though it was clearly a sardonic one. "I guess there are a bunch of things I don't actually know about you."

"Jojo . . ." All he wanted to do was give her a hug, tell her how much he'd missed her, how torturous it had been thinking that she hated him. "May I come in? Just for a few minutes? There are a couple things I'd like to say to you, and, if after that, you still want me to leave, I will. I'd just rather not have this conversation standing on your doorstep."

She didn't say anything. Was this some sort of test? Was she just going to remain silent until he chose a course of action? Which would be what? As the silence stretched, he began to consider his options. He could go in, which perhaps might be what she was hoping, although it could also upset her even more. He could leave, which, he supposed, was just as likely what she wanted, although if he did that, he knew his chances with her were over. Try as he might, he couldn't get a feel for the situation, couldn't decide what the hell it was he was supposed to do. He'd faced a camera and talked to over a billion people, yet now, facing this one woman, he felt paralyzed, utterly unsure of what to do.

The puppy trotted over right then, and sat down in front of Jojo, its tail windshield-wiping across the floor as it looked up at her, mouth open in a doggy grin.

"Well, aren't you just the cutest thing," she said, and she bent down and scooped the puppy up. It immediately began licking her face, and she laughed and hugged the puppy close, and Jack couldn't help but feel a little envious, the words *lucky dog* ratcheting around his brain. Jojo looked at him, as if she could hear his thoughts. "You can come in," she finally said.

All the invitation he needed. Jack slipped inside and closed the door behind him.

"So what's this little guy's name?" she asked.

"Uh . . . well, he doesn't have one yet." He gave her a hopeful look. "I was thinking his new owner might want to decide herself."

That wasn't exactly how he had envisioned the conversation going, and when Jojo narrowed her eyes, Jack wondered if showing up with a puppy had been a wise idea.

"Wait a second," she said. "You're telling me you brought a *puppy* as a peace offering?"

He nodded. "Um . . . yes, yes, that's exactly what I did, I guess. And a few other things." He pulled the passport out of his pocket. "I also have this for you. And this," he added, gesturing to the bag with the two bottles.

"Look at me, being showered in gifts by the American spy." She gave the dog one last squeeze and then set him down. He trotted off, tail wagging, making himself right at home. Jack hoped that was a good sign. She took the passport from him but didn't open it, didn't even look at it. She looked right at him. "Do you know what a shock it was for me to see your face on TV?"

"I know."

"I don't think you do. I don't think you understand at all. You betrayed me, Jack. You lied to me. How am I supposed to trust you if you've been lying to me from the beginning?"

He shook his head. "I know how it looks, I know that you must think that everything has been a lie from the beginning, but it's not like that at all. I was untruthful to you only when I had to be—for your protection. I would never have been able to forgive myself if something happened to you because of me."

"I can take care of myself, Jack," she said, rolling her eyes. I would have much preferred you being honest with me than thinking you need to lie to protect me. I'm not a little girl."

"I know you're not. But I need *you* to know that I am not a spy. I came to China on my own, because I wanted to, because I believe this country has great potential. But there are some roadblocks and I feel honored and fortunate to have been able to take part in helping to remove some of those obstacles." He took a deep breath, trying to gauge her reaction. She was listening to him, at least, so he plunged on. "I'll be honest with you—it is going to be really difficult for me to reconcile what I did and convince myself that it was a good thing if it means losing you in the process. But I realize that there is nothing I can do to change the past and if you truly feel I am not a trustworthy person, then I will accept that. I don't want to, but more than anything, Jojo, I want you to be happy. With or without me. And all of these things I brought—these peace offerings, as you put it—are yours, if you want them. If you don't want the puppy, I'll keep him, but he seems right at home here." Jack nodded to the passport, still in her hand. "And I mean it about that, too."

She finally looked down. She opened the little blue book, flipped to the page with her picture.

"President Sutton was able to get this for you. He asked me if there was anything I needed or wanted, and this was the only thing I could think of. So, you're officially an American diplomat. Your father knows all about it."

She closed the passport. When she looked up at him, he saw that there were tears in her eyes. "I've felt so trapped here," she said.

"Well, now you don't have to. I don't want you to ever feel that way again." He pulled one of the bottles from the bag. "Would you like to share a glass?"

Jojo wiped at her eyes with the back of her hand. "That must be fake," she said. "It can't be real Maotai. It doesn't exist anymore. I've had this kind before; the last bottle was recently sold at an auction for a quarter million dollars."

"Wow." Jack let out a low whistle and looked at the bottle. "I didn't realize it carried such a hefty price tag. Had I known, I might have declined when your dad gave them to me."

Jojo's eyes widened. "Oh my god," she said. "Then this is the best Maotai in the world. If anyone would have some, he would."

"Well, he has two fewer bottles now. Will you have a drink with me?"

"How can I say no to that? Come on." She turned and Jack followed her back to the kitchen, where she took out two small glasses. "I can't believe I have a passport." Jack poured the Maotai, first in her glass, then in his. He gently touched his glass to hers.

"I hope," he said, "that we can continue our relationship. I don't want this to be the end for us. I've missed seeing you, I think about you every single day, and I truly just want you to be happy, Jojo. I am really hoping that includes me being a part of your life."

She held her glass but had not yet taken a sip. He had a feeling this was the moment—she was going to forgive him or tell him to get lost—but leave the Maotai, the passport, and maybe the dog, too. A smile slowly spread across her face.

"I've felt awful, thinking that things were over between us. And I realize that no one is perfect, and I will believe you now, Jack, that you're telling me the truth, and from what I know of you, I do think you were just trying to keep me safe. So long as you understand that I don't need a protector, I'm not some princess locked away in a tower, waiting to be rescued—then yes, I want you to be a part of my life. And this adorable dog that you randomly just showed up with!" She started to laugh. "Who does something like that?" She took a sip, her eyes closing. "Mmm, that is good." She set her glass down, reopening her eyes. "Thank you. And . . . for as mad as I was at you, I want you to know, I also missed you."

Jack smiled. "If that's the case then . . . would you give me a kiss?"

She walked right up to him and gave him a peck on the cheek. "You can have much more than that once we've drunk this bottle of Maotai."

"Fair enough." She picked up her glass and raised it; Jack did the same. "To new beginnings."

He echoed the sentiment, and they clinked glasses. The puppy circled their legs, and then sat down and looked up, first at Jojo, then at Jack.

CHAPTER 3

The unfamiliar sound of a cell phone ringing woke him; for a moment Jack thought it must've been Jojo's phone, but as he came to, he realized that it was coming from the pocket of his pants, which he'd discarded on the floor on his side of the bed.

He delicately moved Jojo's draped arm so he could lean over and get the phone. It was the black phone that he had exclusively used to text with Cooper, from the CIA—no one had ever called him on it before. He slipped out of bed as he picked it up, carefully making his way downstairs so he wouldn't wake Jojo.

"Hello," he said quietly. "It's Jack."

"Jack? Is that you?" It was Cooper. "I can barely hear you, the connection doesn't seem that great."

"Sorry," Jack said, raising his voice a little. "Is that better?"

"Yes, much. So, the president wants to speak with you. He'll be calling in ten minutes and I wanted to give you a head's up."

Jack cleared his throat, trying to push the fog from the Maotai hangover out of his brain. "I appreciate it. Do you know what he's calling about?"

"The trade negotiations with China have completely broken down. It's causing lots of friction politically within the US and the farmers are getting hit pretty hard. China is also suffering. President Sutton wants you to help solve the problem. He thinks you're the right man for the job, and I fully agree with him."

"Okay," Jack said. "Again, I appreciate the forewarning. Just so you know, I'm at Jojo's, and I'll be here to take Sutton's call."

"I know. And that's not a problem."

"Okay. Well, I look forward to the call, and thanks again."

Jack hung up just as Jojo came down the stairs, her hair mussed, a sleepy smile on her face. "I'm sorry," Jack said. "I tried to get to the phone before it woke you."

"I was already half-awake, I think. Just enjoying lying there in your arms. Can we go back up?"

"I would love to, but . . . President Sutton is going to be calling in a few minutes to discuss the trade situation with China. So I probably shouldn't be spooning with you while I'm on that call."

"Probably not."

"But come here." He wrapped his arms around Jojo and gave her a kiss on the forehead. "Just so you know, from here on out, I will keep nothing from you. No secrets whatsoever. Our relationship is more important than anything else."

She looked up at him. "I feel the same way. And I won't keep any secrets from you, either."

They were in the middle of a kiss when the black phone rang again. Jack reluctantly pulled back and answered, realizing, as he did so, he was still naked.

"Hello. Jack Gold."

"Hi Jack. It's Madeline. May I transfer you to the president?"

"Yes, of course."

A moment later, President Sutton was on the line. "Jack," he said. "How are you doing?"

"Couldn't be better, actually," Jack said, winking at Jojo.

"Glad to hear it. Well, listen. The reason for the call is because the trade relations with China have broken down again and I'm a little concerned. I was speaking with Wang Yang yesterday, and we both thought you might be able to help."

"What did you have in mind?"

"We think you can be an honest broker to look out for the interest of both parties. We hoped you could work with all the parties involved and help navigate us to a solution that everyone is happy with. A tall order, I know."

That was putting it mildly. "Mr. President, I'm certainly willing to help out. But, as you said, it's a tall order, and there are many chefs in the kitchen, and huge politics on both sides."

Sutton sighed. "I know, I know. I'm also open to other suggestions. Got any?"

"Let me think about it. As I said, I'm more than happy to help. But we want to go into this prepared, and a framework for discussions and decision-making needs to be formulated first and agreed upon." Jack could sense Sutton nodding his head, so he continued. "If you and Wang Yang think I should be involved, then I would put together the framework and visit both of you to discuss it. Only if there is agreement on both sides would proceeding make sense. Each of you will have to sign off."

"That sounds like it could take a while. What's your estimate? We don't want this dragging out any longer than is necessary."

"Of course. I can visit Wang Yang next week, and then go directly to Washington. I think a reasonable estimate to get the framework side completed is about a month. But, that really depends upon you and Wang Yang."

"That's great, Jack. I'll let Wang Yang know. I'm thrilled that you're back together with Jojo. We'd love to see her at the White House. Bring her along."

Jack tried to bite back his smile. Here he was, being congratulated by the president about the status of his relationship . . . all while he stood naked in his girlfriend's apartment. "Thank you, sir," Jack said. "I'll coordinate things through Cooper. I'll see you soon."

"Excellent. Thank you, Jack. Enjoy your day."

Jack said goodbye and hung up. The second the phone was away from his ear, Jojo burst out laughing. "You do realize," she gasped, "that you're standing here naked, talking with the President of the United States?"

"Funny you should say that, because I just had that same thought."

"So, what did he have to say?"

"He wants me to help out with the trade negotiations between China and America. The trade war is hurting everyone, especially China." And it was true. Companies were leaving, China couldn't purchase semiconductors, and Heidan Enterprises was blocked from using all sorts of American technology for its phones, including Google's operating system. It was a mess and impacting GDP. "I'm going to see your dad next week to see if I can get his agreement on some terms, then I'll go to Washington to meet with Sutton. Would you join me?"

"Well, seeing as I have a passport that will let me do that . . . Of course!" She looked down, at the puppy who was circling her legs. "I think this guy probably needs to go for a walk. Also . . . what are we going to do with him while we're away? I mean, he can come with us to see my dad, but I don't think a cross-continent journey will be good for him at this age."

Jack regarded the black and white ball of fuzz. "That's true," he said, "and I hadn't thought about that ahead of time . . ."

"I have some friends who wouldn't mind watching him, but seeing as he's so new, I think we should bring him with us to my dad's, and he can stay there until we get back from Washington. My dad loves dogs, too—he'll be thrilled to see this guy." Jojo leaned down and picked up the puppy, who immediately tried to start licking her face. "You need a name," she said. "We can't let you go without a name for much longer."

While Jojo went to get dressed, Jack texted Cooper on the black phone, letting him know that he and Jojo wanted to visit Beijing and see President Wang next week, at his convenience. Cooper texted back to him immediately and said he would arrange it. Jack looked down at the puppy, who was sitting near his feet, looking up at him, one ear cocked up, as if waiting for his next instruction.

"You're a good boy," Jack said. "Let's take you out for a walk and then we'll get you your breakfast. Guess I should go get dressed, too."

Jack dressed quickly and stepped outside with Jojo and the dog. They walked a few blocks, and Jack used the plastic bag he had with him to clean up after the puppy had taken care of his business. They turned the corner and the dog stopped, ears pricked forward. He barked once, then again. Jack looked to see what had caught the dog's attention, but only saw a dark green Mini Cooper.

"Is he barking at the car?" Jojo asked. She gave the leash a little tug. "Come on, you. It's just a parked car."

But the puppy only stood there, looking at the car with his head cocked slightly to the side. Jojo laughed.

"Mini," she said. She looked at Jack. "What do you think? Is that a good name?"

Jack smiled. "Aren't Mini Coopers the car men in China usually get for their mistresses? Maybe we should call him *Ernai* instead." He snickered. Ernai meant "second milk" and was a less than kind nickname that was sometimes given to a mistress.

Jojo made a face. "Oh yeah, that would go over really well, if I have to yell *Ernai* down the street if he ever got out."

"You have a point," Jack said. "Though it would be funny." He looked down at the dog, who was now focused on a leaf that was skittering down the sidewalk. "Mini it is," he said.

CHAPTER 4

For their trip to Beijing, Jack, Jojo, and Mini were guests at the same hotel Jack had stayed in when he had first returned to China after the Control Center broadcast. Davis had picked them up earlier in a black SUV at Jojo's apartment and drove them to the airport. There had been additional security, driving in front and in back of them, because, as Davis had informed them, the word was out that they were together, and people knew where they lived.

Still, Jack couldn't help but be excited to travel with Jojo. And she had seemed equally taken by their plush travel accommodations, this time in a Gulfstream G650 ER. Their plan was to have dinner with Wang Yang that evening, and then Jack would have a more official meeting to discuss the framework he'd been working on all week, the following day.

It was Jim who showed them into their suite, once again in the vacant hotel. There were fresh flowers and a large bowl of assorted fruit on the table in the entryway, two large windows facing the garden, and, beyond that, a pool. Their luggage was already there, waiting by the door to the bedroom.

"Thank you, Jim," Jack said. "Everything looks great. I think we're just going to rest for a while."

"Let me know if there is anything you need," Jim said.

Jojo walked over to the windows and looked out. "What a lovely garden. It reminds me of the one that I had growing up, where I used to grow watermelon with my dad. I bet they would grow beautifully here."

He came up behind her and wrapped his arms around her waist, rested his chin on her shoulder as they both looked out the window. "The garden is nice but you know what I thought looked even nicer? That jacuzzi bathtub they have in here. Would you like to join me?"

She craned her neck around and gave him a kiss. "I would love to."

He went into the bathroom to start the bath. The tub was polished granite, with gently sloping sides that were perfect for reclining against. It was so large it would take a while to fill up, so Jack fiddled with the faucet, getting the water to the perfect temperature. He poured in some L'Occitane bath salts and then went out to the other room.

Jojo was stretched out on the bed, looking at something on her phone. She put the phone down when Jack came over and lay down next to her. He kissed her, gently at first, and then with more force, as she kissed him back, entwining her legs around his. He cupped the side of her face, ran his thumb along her jawline, then lower, caressing her neck, then lower, to her collarbone, then lower, to her breast, which he squeezed gently as he continued to kiss her. She groaned and pressed herself against him harder, and then he realized that the bathwater was still running.

"Let's continue this in the bathtub," he said, reluctantly breaking away. "But first, I'll help you get undressed."

She let him slide off her tight black pants, and just the sight of her long, shapely legs filled him with excitement. She pulled her shirt off, reached around and undid her bra. "Let me help you with your clothes," she said, reaching for his belt.

The bathtub was almost filled when they went in. Jack tested the water, which was the perfect temperature, and smelled fragrant, like lavender. They carefully climbed in, Jack first, then Jojo.

"Are you comfortable?" he asked. He couldn't imagine being more comfortable, submerged in the hot water that felt like liquid satin, the woman he loved leaning against him.

"I am." She turned so she was straddling him. "But now I'm even more comfortable." She wiggled her hips back and forth a little, until he felt himself slide into her. He inhaled sharply and let his eyes close.

"Okay," he said. "I'm more than comfortable."

He ran his hands up and down her sides as she leaned down and kissed him; they moved in easy synchronicity, it was like a dance they both knew fluently, a dance he would be happy to partake in any time.

*   *   *

Several hours later, they were in the back of gray Audi, on their way to Zhongnanhai. As happened last time, Davis was following behind, but would not be allowed to enter the compound. Still, Jack appreciated just knowing that he was nearby.

It seemed unlikely, though. As they drove, Jack asked Jojo what she thought tonight's dinner might be like. She smiled.

"Are you nervous, Jack Gold?" she said. "I think that's adorable."

"It's not every night I dine with a head of state."

"I have a feeling you'll be just fine. Usually when I dine with my dad, a few family friends drop by to say hello. It's always pretty laid back; I think everyone will have a good time."

When they arrived there, they were escorted through elegant, well-lit corridors, showcasing the priceless art hanging from the walls. Though they had an attendant with them, as Jack had the first time he came here, Jojo seemed quite familiar with the place.

They arrived in a room with two large, round tables, draped with linen and set with small Chinese dishes and rice bowls and spoons. Jack glanced at Jojo. This did not look like a casual dinner.

Then again, they weren't dressed casually either—Jojo wore a form-fitting black dress with three-quarter length sleeves and a plunging V-neck, and he had chosen a navy suit with a red tie. He reached for her hand right as Wang Yang walked in.

Jojo gave Jack's hand a quick squeeze before she let go to greet her father. In China, fathers did not hug their daughters, rather, she took both of his hands in hers, which was a common way for Chinese parents to greet their children.

They began talking in a Suzhou dialect, though Jack didn't mind not being able to participate in the conversation, as he enjoyed just seeing Jojo getting to interact with her dad, the easy way their conversation flowed, whatever it was they were talking about.

Finally, Wang Yang looked at Jack. "Welcome back to Beijing. It's good to see you."

He came over and they shook hands. "Good to see you too," Jack said.

"Why don't we sit down."

Jack nodded, but waited until Wang Yang indicated what seat he should take; in a situation like this, Chinese seating etiquette was always taken seriously.

Wang motioned for Jack to sit at the place directly facing the door, the guest of honor's seat. Jojo sat to Jack's left; Wang sat to his right. Jack had not been expecting such an arrangement.

"What would you like to drink?" Wang asked.

Jack looked at Jojo. "Maotai?"

"Of course," she said with a smile.

"I should've known." Wang spoke to one of the attendants and a moment later, glasses and a bottle of the Maotai that Jojo had thought didn't exist anymore were brought out. Once the glasses were filled, Wang raised his, looking right at Jack.

"To friendship."

They toasted and drank the small amount that had been poured. The glasses were immediately refilled, and now it was Jack's turn. He looked at Jojo, then at her father. "To family."

When it was Jojo's turn, she held up her glass, her gaze going first to her father, then to Jack. "To the two men in my life."

Their glasses were filled once more. "To watermelons," Jack said. Wang looked back at him in confusion.

"Did you know," Jack said, "that even though they don't look like it, watermelons are berries? The place we're staying in has a great garden and looks perfect for growing watermelons, just like you did with Jojo, many years ago." He paused, a realization suddenly forming. "My guess is that you were hoping we would move there."

Wang frowned, and for a moment Jack feared he had said the wrong thing, or perhaps shouldn't have said anything at all. But then his brow unfurled and he chuckled, a bit self-effacingly, it seemed.

"Am I that obvious," he said. "But . . . you're correct."

Jojo's eyebrows shot up. "He is?"

"He is."

They tipped their glasses and drank the Maotai.

"Actually," Jack said, putting his empty glass down, "it's not a bad idea. The bottom floor could be converted into your studio—it's big enough. The light is good. Plenty of room for our dog outside . . . and I bet we can convince President Wang to help with the watermelon planting."

Now Jojo had the frown on her face, her eyes going back and forth from Jack to her father. "Wait a second. I feel like the two of you are in on something I'm only just finding out about now. Which is fine, except it also sounds like it involves me, so I think I should have a say."

"It's a nice gesture by your dad," Jack said. "And we weren't in on it or anything—I think we just caught on sooner than he planned."

"More like *you* caught on sooner," Jojo said. "I'm just trying to enjoy my Maotai."

"Jack is correct," Wang Yang said. "The security issue is real. The reason family members of senior party officials live in Zhongnanhai is largely for safety. There are people who are very angry at Jack. Those feelings aren't likely to dissipate any time soon. And Jojo, you're the daughter of the president. Compounding this is the now public knowledge that you are both together, which has increased your visibility. And you currently live in different locations and thus must travel back and forth quite a bit."

Jack felt Jojo grab his hand underneath the table. She gave it a squeeze, and though no words were issued, clearly she wanted him to hold off on saying anything.

"Okay," she said. "We'll think about it."

Wang smiled. "Let's have one more drink before the others arrive."

Jack stayed seated, like Jojo and Wang Yang did, as people started to show up. The guests came over to greet them and shake hands; mostly they were family friends and people working in Wang Yang's administration. Zhao Lihong was there, and Jack continued to be amazed at how much more at ease the man looked now that he had been relieved of his presidential duties.

"Welcome to Beijing," he said to Jack. "I hope to see more of you."

"Likewise," Jack said.

Zhao smiled and looked at Jojo. "Last time Jack was here, he showed us your new passport. Will you be using it soon?"

"When Jack goes to meet with President Sutton. I thought I'd tag along."

Zhao raised his glass. "To a successful journey, then."

As guests arrived, so did the food. It was classical Beijing fare—there were sliced cucumbers in vinegar, eggplant, watercress, steamed fish, duck, spicy chicken, and dumplings. Jack savored the tart and savory flavors, so different than that of Shanghainese cuisine. After he and Jojo had their fill, he stood up with her and they went around and mingled. People were curious about him and inquired about what he did for work, how long he had been living in China, how did he and Jojo meet? But no one brought up the Control Center, and Jack appreciated that.

Eventually, they made their way back to their seats. Jack looked at Jojo. He wanted to give her a kiss, badly, but he knew how inappropriate that would be. Instead, he gave her a smile and refilled her glass. He raised his. "To our future, and our journey together."

"To both of you," Wang said. He stood, holding his glass, and the conversation around them died down. "I'd like to make a final toast." He waited until everyone had a full glass. "You've all had the chance to meet Jack Gold, and everyone knows my daughter, Jojo. I would just like to tell you two how happy I am for the both of you, and I am certain you have many years of great happiness together ahead of you. To Jojo and Jack." He lifted his glass, and everyone else did the same.

"To Jojo and Jack!"

It was a strange but good feeling to have such positive affirmation from people he barely even knew about his relationship. He looked at Jojo and gave her a wink, and she grinned back at him.

*   *   *

They had a slow start the next morning that required lots of coffee. Jack took Mini out for a quick walk before Jojo was awake, and he was definitely hungover, though it wasn't awful.

When he returned, he found Jojo was up, so they went downstairs for breakfast, where they dined on onion cake with fried egg and spicy chili oil, which, in Jack's opinion, was the best hangover food. Properly prepared, it was actually one of his favorite Beijing meals, though it was hard to find elsewhere in China.

After breakfast, they returned to their room. Jojo took a shower, so Jack checked online about the latest on the so-called trade war between America and China. There was only one new article in the *South China Morning Post*, which stated America was claiming that China was still selling fentanyl to the U.S., which China denied.

His black phone beeped, and Jack reached over to read the message from Cooper: *Security is becoming a bigger issue. We are working with Beijing to address. Wanted you to be aware.*

Jack frowned. Of course that wasn't the news that he wanted to hear, but he understood, and appreciated being kept in the loop. He texted back, asking if Cooper thought it was wise for he and Jojo to just move into this hotel, as Wang Yang had hoped. Cooper's response came quickly: *That would be a good idea. And it would help us. But ultimately it's your call.*

He considered what it might be like, actually living here. Certainly there were far worse places to live, and also—it meant he and Jojo would be living together. Which to some might seem a bit soon, but in Jack's mind, he was more than ready. He didn't want to rush Jojo, though.

He heard the water in the bathroom go off, and then a few minutes later she emerged, one towel wrapped around her body, another around her head like a turban.

"I have a question," Jack said.

"And I would love to hear it." She let the towel wrapped around her body fall away as she dug through her suitcase for her clothes.

"Well, I can't ask you like *this*," Jack said, thoroughly enjoying the view. "I mean, I don't even remember what the question *was* . . ."

Jojo unwrapped the towel on her head and her damp hair tumbled past her shoulders. She pulled a black t-shirt on. "That better?"

Jack groaned. "Not really . . ."

"What was this question of yours?"

"My what? Oh yeah. Question. If you could tear everything out of this downstairs area and create a space to your liking what would you do?"

She stepped into a pair of black lacy underwear Jack hoped he'd be able to help her out of later. Then a pair of jeans. A simple outfit but she looked stunning.

"I would indeed tear everything out, including the ceiling and the wallpaper. The floor would need to be removed. If there is authentic wood there, I'd keep it; otherwise, I'd pour in cement. The lighting would have to change. The walls would be painted white. We could put in some large Persian carpets on this side so it'd be comfortable. The other side would be my studio. The wall between looks like it could be torn down, too. Overall, I'd say it would be an industrial design, which would open the space up nicely, don't you agree?"

Jack laughed. "I was thinking you were going to tell me that you needed to think about it first."

"Well, I haven't seen the kitchen yet. But . . . why are you asking?"

"How do you feel about moving in together?"

If she was surprised at the question, she didn't show it, which Jack hoped was a good sign.

"I think there are people who feel *we* would be safer if we were living together. So there's that to consider," Jack said. "Though if I'm to be honest, it's that I just like the idea of being able to wake up next to you every morning."

She smiled slowly. "I think that sounds lovely." Mini circled at her feet. "And what do you think? Would you like to live here, too? You've certainly made yourself right at home, rascal."

The more he thought about the idea, the more it seemed like the right choice. Not just because he wanted to take this next step in his relationship with Jojo, but also because of the multitude of security concerns. All signals were pointing them in this direction.

"I think we should do it," Jojo said. "That is, if you want to."

"Nothing would make me happier. Should I tell your father today when I see him?"

"Sure, why not? He'll be thrilled."

It would be good to have some positive news to deliver to Wang today, in case he wasn't as thrilled with Jack's proposal as Jack was hoping he'd be.

He went and prepared for his meeting. Before he left, he gave Jojo a kiss goodbye. "Have a good day, and I'll see you when you get back," she said, smoothing the lapels of his jacket.

"I'm already looking forward to it," he said. He said goodbye to Mini and then departed, thinking how nice it would be to get to come home to Jojo every day.

Davis was waiting out front and Jack hopped into the black SUV.

"They've agreed to let us drive you," Davis said as they pulled away from the hotel.

"That's good," Jack said. "I'd much prefer to go with you. I heard from Cooper that there are some security issues. Any details you're able to share?"

"We've been hearing a variety of things, but there is one credible group that is not happy with what you did, and with President Wang. Whether or not they're going to act is another story, but we want to be ready for anything. It's on the Chinese side, so our information is limited. But we're taking it very seriously."

Jack nodded. "Well, I think Jojo and I are probably going to move into the hotel. That should make things easier, right?"

"Absolutely. And hey—seems like pretty nice living quarters."

Jack wondered about who this unhappy, credible group was, though there was a part of him that didn't want to know all the details, if for no other reason than he didn't want it to overshadow every aspect of his life. Perhaps that was a foolish stance, but he trusted Davis and Cooper and the security team, and he also knew Wang Yang would do everything in his power to ensure his daughter was safe.

"I'm getting a little more used to coming here," Jack said as they approached the entrance of Zhongnanhai.

"I bet you are," Davis said. "I'll be out here, as always."

This time, Jack was escorted by the same man and woman who had previously taken him to meet with Wang Yang, though instead they went to a conference room, elegantly decorated with traditional Chinese art.

Wang was already there, with two other people from his administration.

"Jack, thank you for agreeing to help out with our trade discussions. This is Wei Li and Shen Huang. They've been appointed to assist." Jack smiled and introduced himself to the man and woman before they all took their seats at the large table. "So," Wang said, "you know the current situation. America has placed tariffs on hundreds of billion dollars of Chinese goods. This is decreasing the demand for products, and in some cases, companies are moving out of China. The demands America is making on China are attacking the country's pride. China does not simply do what other countries tell it to do." He paused. "What do you think about the situation?"

Jack took a deep breath. He had expected this question, but still knew that he needed to word things delicately. "First of all, I am not here as an advocate of America. I care equally that both countries thrive economically." He paused, wanting to emphasize the point. "There are some challenges, that's certainly true. Everything seems to play out via Twitter and the press, which enflames the situation. Second, America has some fundamental misunderstandings about economics." Shen Huang, seated to the right of Wang, smirked when Jack said this. "If China produces very inexpensive steel and Americans lose jobs, America still gains from lower costs for anything made with that steel. Sutton and his people need to read the book I shared with everyone, the one by Milton Friedman."

Jack watched as Shen Huang and Wei Li exchanged glances; he had insulted America, but he had done it on purpose. And it was also true—many people in America would benefit from reading that book.

"Regarding letting Heidan do business," Jack continued, "America claims national security concerns. I don't believe this. In the late 1980s, the U.S. banned the sale of PCs to China with the argument that it is *dual use technology*, meaning the PC could be used for military use as well. If China wants to have state-owned enterprises, it's the same thing. America has an industrial policy; so does China. The form of it is just different. The influences within both countries are just too great, making the reaching of an agreement impossible. For example, Sutton has to look out for farmers, since they're an important part of his electoral base. But, as I said, there are too many people with different interests. Too many cooks in the kitchen."

Wang pulled a pack of his cigarettes from his pocket, extracted one, and then pushed the pack over to Jack. "Too many cooks in the kitchen," he repeated. "That sounds about right. So how do we get some of these cooks out of the kitchen?"

Jack took his time, lighting the cigarette, taking a long, pleasant drag. It wasn't that he was thinking because he didn't know what to say—he was trying to determine the ideal way to lay out what he thought was their best option.

He exhaled a plume of smoke. "I propose a single team be formed," he began. "The team will be composed of three people from China and three people from America. And myself. I will guide the team through all the issues, with the assistance of outside experts. If everyone on the team—all seven of us—can come to an agreement, will you agree to abide by the terms? Providing America agrees as well?"

Wang smoked his cigarette and exchanged looks with Wei Li and Shen Huang. For several moments, no one said anything.

"The stated purpose of the team will be to have a plan that maximizes the economic benefit to all," Jack said. "That maximizes the benefit to each nation and its citizens."

Wang stubbed out his cigarette. "Are there any other conditions?"

"The team members cannot report back to anyone about anything. And, I have the authority to remove team members from either side, at my complete discretion, should I find it necessary."

"How long will it take?"

"Probably no more than a few months, full-time. Americans need to be re-educated on a number of things, as I've mentioned. The same will be the case for the Chinese. Trust needs to be built. You will have three people there. You will not be happy with everything that comes out of the agreement. But, it will be in China's interest, for sure."

"Seven people must all agree and then the nations must abide by the agreement," Wang said. Jack nodded. "Sutton will have to agree to the same framework and terms."

Jack reached down and opened his briefcase, pulled out a plastic sleeve. "Here you go," he said, sliding a copy to each of them. "This is a summary of the framework and terms. I'm hoping both you and Sutton will review, agree to it, and sign it." Wang glanced at the paper.

"I apologize I didn't write this in Chinese. My written Chinese is horrible."

Wang leaned back in his chair and looked at his two associates. "Would you excuse us for a moment?" he said.

Wei Li and Shen Huang immediately stood and exited the room. Wang looked down at the paper in front of him, then at Jack. "Do you think this will work?"

"There will be some tricky things, like enforcement mechanisms. But China has a big incentive in the IP arena since it now needs to globally protect its own innovation."

"Has Sutton seen this?"

Jack shook his head. "No. I'm playing this straight down the middle. No favoritism whatsoever."

Wang looked pleased to hear that. "How will Sutton react?"

"He'll be concerned that some aspect of an agreement might cause harm to his constituents. Ultimately, though, he'll reason that such an agreement will be great for the stock market. That'll be good for him."

"What type of person do you think will be best to select?"

"Someone with an excellent understanding of economics, ideally."

Wang looked down at the paper again, his brow furrowed. Jack sat back, feeling good about the way things had so far gone. He knew neither side would be completely happy with what he had come up with, but there was no option, as far as Jack knew, that would completely satisfy both sides one hundred percent.

"Obviously, I'm going to need a little time to think about this," Wang said. "But I think we're on the right track here. I appreciate your continued effort, Jack; there is no doubt in my mind that you're true to your word and are not taking sides in this."

"Thank you," Jack said. "Both countries have a great deal to offer, and both could prosper. That's what I'd like to see." He paused. "And . . . not to deviate too much from the current topic, but . . . I do have some good news."

"Oh?"

"Jojo and I have decided to take you up on the offer to move into the hotel."

The slightly pensive look that had been on Wang's face for the majority of the meeting turned into the biggest grin Jack had yet to see on the man's face.

"Did you?" he exclaimed. "Why, that's excellent news! I'm so happy to hear it."

"It will probably come as little surprise that Jojo would like to remodel a bit so she can continue her work there."

"Certainly."

"She already knows just how she wants to modify things."

Wang shook his head slightly, the smile still on his face. "I would expect nothing less." He leaned toward Jack. "But between you and me—it'll probably look much better once she's done with it."

"I agree," Jack said.

"We'll send someone by tomorrow so they can talk to her about what she wants to do. When do you leave for DC?"

"Tomorrow afternoon."

"Jojo must be ecstatic."

"She's definitely looking forward to it. I am, too. I mean, I'm excited to be going back there with her. Would you like me to pass any message along to Sutton?"

"No need; I speak to him periodically. He's also looking forward to your visit, and meeting Jojo. It should be a fun trip."

"I hope so," Jack said. "I'll be looking forward to getting both of your signatures on this framework, though I suspect both you and Sutton will want a little time to think things through. Jojo and I were thinking we might travel around a bit while we're there, see some of the sights."

"She'll love that. And it will be a good time to get your new home ready for your return. Can we help moving your things from Shanghai to Beijing?"

"Possibly," Jack said, "though that's really a question Jojo would need to answer."

"Well, if she'd like the assistance, it's no hassle. Anything she needs, you tell her to let me know."

Jack smiled. "She probably already knows that, but I will certainly pass the message along."

"Then I think we're finished here, for now," Wang said. He stood, and so did Jack. "Safe travels if I don't talk to you before you leave."

"Thank you," Jack said, and he wondered, before he left, if the president of China was going to be his future father-in-law.

*   *   *

Jack returned to the hotel, eager to see Jojo, who he found in the hotel's lounge, sitting on a leather chair, looking at the screen of her laptop.

"Honey, I'm home," he said.

Jojo stood up and walked over, gave him kiss. "Welcome home, dear. I'm just working on a detailed list of everything that needs to be done. Otherwise, things will get messed up. The kitchen looks pretty good, actually. And I've decided to convert one of the rooms upstairs into an office for us."

Jack smiled, liking the idea of the two of them sharing an office. "Your dad said he'd send some people by tomorrow morning. He also said he'd be happy to help in any way, like if we need assistance moving everything from Shanghai, but I told him you would be the person to talk to about that. I figured, if we took some time while we're in America and did a little sightseeing and relaxing, things might be done here by the time we arrive back."

"I like how you think," Jojo said. "But will they really be done that quickly?"

"I guess that depends on just how detailed these notes of yours are."

"Well, they're pretty detailed." Jojo paused. "Is that what he said, my father?" "*Anything?*"

"I'm pretty sure those were the exact words he used. *Anything she needs.*"

"I think it makes sense to ask him if Mini can stay with him while we're on our trip. He might act put out by it, but I know when we come back, he'll probably not want to give Mini back!"

Jack smiled down at the pup, who had trotted over and was wrestling with a stuffed toy frog. He felt a little bad, getting the dog and then having to leave him so soon, but there was no way they could bring him with them to America.

"I guess that's going to be our best option."

Jack's phone beeped, and he pulled it out of his pocket. It was a WeChat message from Joshua.

Back in Beijing, it read. *Just wanted to check in. Let me know next time you're around and we can get together for a drink. Might also be down in Shanghai in the next few weeks.*

"It's my friend Joshua," he said. "He's asking when's the next time I'll be in Beijing; he wants to get together for a drink. You'll like him."

Jojo had gone back to typing on her laptop. "Did I meet him already?"

"I don't think so. Maybe at Bar No. 3, if you did. I should get in touch with Ari, too. I'll ask Joshua if he's heard from him. I know we're leaving tomorrow, but would you be up for meeting with Joshua tonight for drinks? It won't be a late night or anything, but I think it would be nice to see him, and the timing sure seems perfect."

"Sure. I'm more than curious to meet the rest of the people you under-took this mission with. Where did you want to go?"

Jack was about to suggest somewhere like the Jianguo Hotel, but then it dawned on him that they were staying there, in a hotel all to themselves

"Why don't we just invite him over here?"

"Fine by me. I mean, we could definitely throw a serious sort of party here."

He texted an invitation to Joshua, who replied back it would be perfect, he plans to meet up with David later that evening, so he could stop by beforehand and have a drink.

A few minutes after six that evening, Jack received a text from Joshua, letting him know that he had arrived. Jojo was getting changed, so Jack went down to meet him.

"Hey," Jack said. They hugged, clapping each other on the back.

"Good to see you," Joshua said. "Man. What a coincidence that you're here! And you're staying in this place?"

"We are," Jack said as they headed into the hotel. "We have the whole place to ourselves, in fact, so thanks for being our first guest." He paused. "Jojo and I are actually going to be moving in here."

"No kidding?" Joshua's eyes were wide as he looked around. "Wow. Good for you guys. This place is nice. Really nice."

"Jojo's not a fan; she has all sort of renovation plans in the works. But she has an incredible eye for that sort of thing, so I'm sure whatever she's planning will look great."

"And if it doesn't . . . just pretend you love it!" Joshua laughed. "I had an aunt who liked to think of herself as this great interior decorator, but I think she was actually color blind. Either way, everyone in the family knew that whenever we went over to their place, to act like Aunt Val's redecorating was just perfect."

Jojo was just coming out of the bedroom, in a pair of turquoise leggings and a long black t-shirt dress.

"Good evening," she said, smiling at Joshua. "I'm Jojo."

"Joshua. So nice to finally meet you!"

"Joshua is from Israel and knows your dad," Jack said to Jojo. "He's the one who filmed me when I was in the broadcasting center."

"So *you're* the one who's responsible for broadcasting my man's face to the entire population of China!"

"Sincere apologies," Joshua said, "but you have to admit, he did such a good job!" He looked at Jojo more closely. "Do I know you from somewhere? You look familiar." He glanced at Jack. "You said I know her dad?"

"My dad is Wang Yang," she said.

Joshua's mouth fell open. "Oh my gosh," he said. "I didn't realize that!"

"Why don't we get a drink," Jack said. "And take this conversation over to the couch."

They decided on a bottle of Taittinger champagne, and immediately upon sitting down, Jojo turned to Joshua.

"Tell me what happened. What *really* happened. I want all the details."

Joshua took a sip of his champagne and looked at Jack. "You mean you didn't fill her in?"

"I told her some. But I don't want to have any secrets with Jojo, so if you'd like to give her your version . . . by all means."

"I can do that," Joshua said. "But let's start a little further back. China was buying oil from Iran, and Iran used this money to support terrorists. Iran has also threatened to annihilate Israel. At the same time, America was pissed off about China stealing all sorts of stuff, killing CIA agents, and being dishonest with the Chinese people. So, a plan was formulated—led by Israel, with American support—to use the CCTV Headquarters to have someone speak to all of China and share documents."

Jack took a sip of his champagne and watched Jojo's face as she listened intently to Joshua. It was hard to tell what she was thinking, though he hoped, if anything, Joshua's words would lay to rest any lingering doubts she might have had that Jack was a spy.

"And then Ari ended up meeting Jack and eventually asking him if he'd like to help and he agreed. He didn't even really know what the plan was at the time; he just wanted to help China. When it came time to enter the Control Center, the person who we had picked to speak got into a scuffle with a guard and ended up incapacitated. So, Jack stepped in and really saved the day."

"Oh, stop it," Jack said. "He's exaggerating."

"Not by much."

"Wait a second," Jojo said, "but how did you even get into the center?"

"We were on a 'tour' of the building. We knew where we needed to go. Then, the alarms went off. There was a biohazard announcement, and everyone had to vacate. I made the video of Jack and then we went to the Control Center to upload it."

Jojo raised her eyebrows and looked at Jack. "That must've been intense. And you went into this whole thing thinking that you weren't going to have to say anything?"

"That was the plan." Jack paused. He knew Jojo wasn't interested in politics, but he wondered what her thoughts were about all of this. Was Joshua's retelling of this making her understand why they did it? Or was she now seeing him in a different light? "Do you think we did the right thing?"

"The whole thing is very complicated. All things considered, I would say it *seems* like everything went pretty well."

Joshua smiled. "That's my feeling, too. It didn't go exactly how we thought it would, but we still managed to pull it off."

"And it seems like it worked out. My father is president. Jack is working closely with America and China to try to find a good compromise. But there could be ramifications later on, and I would just hate if something bad happened. Not that I want to be thinking like that. Ultimately, though, I know that you guys had good intentions. You weren't being selfish—you were trying to help people. How could I disagree with that?"

Jojo held her glass up. "To both of you, and Ari, and anyone else who helped you guys carry this out successfully."

Jack held his glass up and then took a drink, feeling as if a burden of sorts had been lifted. He knew that he'd eventually have to explain things to Jojo, and having Joshua here to help certainly made it easier.

"Although," she said, putting her glass down, "I hope you guys also realize how dangerous that was. I mean, you could've been killed, or imprisoned."

Jack reached over and took her hand. "That was something we were aware of," he said. "We didn't go into this thinking we were invincible."

"I'm just realizing it," Jojo said, "just how much trouble you guys could've gotten in. I'm beyond relieved that didn't happen."

"Me, too." Jack reached for the bottle of champagne and poured himself a little more, then topped Jojo's glass, then Joshua's off. "How's the jet fuel business?" he asked, wanting to move on to a different topic.

"Quite well, actually. I have some other Israeli businesses that want me to assist them in coming to China, so that's good. Oh, and . . . I wanted to wait for the right time to tell you this, but you have an open invitation to visit Israel. The president would like to personally thank you for your role in everything."

"Wow," Jack said. "Really?"

"Really."

Jack glanced at Jojo, who had a big smile on her face. "That sounds like fun! You should definitely do that, Jack."

"We'd love to go—it would be an incredible opportunity. Tomorrow we head out to DC to see Sutton and try to resolve this trade spat. We're going to stay in the US for a little while, but after that, yes, it would be great."

"Excellent. And I know Ari wants to see you. He and Mary are visiting her family right now, but he told me to tell you he'll be in touch at some point."

"I've been wanting to talk to him," Jack said. "Maybe when I'm back from the US we can all get together for a drink."

"That would be great," Joshua said.

"Yes, great, so long as the three of you don't start scheming any more plans!" Jojo said, laughing.

Joshua hung out for a little while longer and then headed out to go meet up with David. Jack was glad he'd been able to stop by, but was also eager for an early night, since they had a long day of traveling ahead of them tomorrow.

CHAPTER 5

While in DC, Jack and Jojo were staying at the W Hotel, with Tom and Denis working their security detail. They had dinner plans that evening with Sutton and his wife, Cam, but before that, they had a few hours to relax in their hotel suite together.

"This view is incredible," Jojo said, gazing out the window. Jack came up behind her.

"It is unusual to have such a view," he said, pointing. "If you look, you can see the Washington Monument, and over to the right is the White House."

Jojo looked, her brow furrowing. "You're right!" she exclaimed. "There they are. Wow."

"You'll get a much better view of the White House shortly. I was thinking a shower might be in order first."

Jojo turned and put her arms around him. "I think that's your best idea yet."

*   *   *

At 6:30 p.m. sharp, Davis came and picked them up. Instead of exiting via the main entrance, though, Davis led them through the gym, where there was another, less visible, exit.

"Are there reporters or other people out front?" Jack asked, once they were in the back of the SUV, heading toward the White House.

Davis shook his head. "No, and we'd like to keep it that way, so just taking some precautions. Probably can't keep it a secret forever, but we'd like to try for as long as possible."

Jojo shifted in the seat, jittered her leg against his, shifted again. She looked nervous, so Jack put his hand on her leg.

"Everything okay?" he asked.

"Yeah," she said. "I'm just a little nervous, I guess. It's not every day you go to dinner with the President of the United States! Is this really happening?"

Jack found her nervousness endearing, particularly in light of the fact her own father was a respected politician, and now the president of China. And she looked so stunning in her full-length, floral print dress that he really didn't think she had a single thing to feel nervous about. Still, he himself sometimes felt as if he were going to wake up and realize this whole surreal experience had just been a dream.

"You have no reason to be nervous," he said. "You're incredible. And I think you'll really hit it off with Sutton's wife, Cam. She's half-Vietnamese, and she speaks French. Before she was First Lady, she had a successful career as a fashion model and she started a jewelry company." He smiled. "And that concludes your briefing."

"Oh, great! A fashion model and a jewelry designer. I feel even *more* nervous!" But Jojo laughed, and that, to Jack, was a good sign.

Upon entering the White House, Jack saw a familiar face. "Cooper!" he said. They shook hands. "Good to see you. I'd like you to meet Jojo."

"Pleasure," Cooper said, shaking her hand. "Great to see you both on this side of the Atlantic. Now, to get this little bit of housekeeping out of the way—may I have your phones please? And, I'd like to meet with you both tomorrow at ten a.m., before your eleven o'clock meeting with the president and trade group."

"Sure," Jack said as he handed Cooper his phones.

"It shouldn't take long, but I'd like to discuss security-related issues."

"Anything I should be concerned about?"

"At this moment? No. Enjoy your evening and we'll brief you tomorrow."

Davis led them to the president's dining room, on the second floor. It was an elegant room, with walls covered in a yellow silk damask. There was a crystal chandelier above a round table set for four. There was also a large fireplace that featured an ornately framed mirror on its mantel, and as Jack caught sight of his reflection in it, he couldn't help but again feel like he was going to wake up at any moment and realize this was all a dream.

But then Cam entered, from a different door at the other side of the room. She was tall and wore a flattering rose-colored dress with a V-neck and three-quarter length sleeves.

"Good evening," she said, a warm smile on her face as she shook first Jack's hand, then Jojo's. "Jack, so nice to finally meet you in person. And you must be Jojo! A pleasure. Come, let's go sit down on the sofa for a few minutes."

They followed Cam over to the sofa in the corner of the room. "How was the flight over?"

"It was quite comfortable," Jojo said. "We really flew in style! There was a bed and the food was great."

The door opened again, and Jack looked, expecting to see Sutton; instead, it was a staff member there to take their drink orders. Jack and Jojo each ordered a glass of Chardonnay, and Cam ordered pomegranate juice.

After the staff left, Jojo said something to Cam in French, and Cam's eyes lit up. She responded in French, and the two began an animated conversation that Jack understood not one word of.

Not that he minded listening to two beautiful women speak in a language that was undeniably pleasing to hear. When the door opened again, though, and he saw that this time, it was Sutton, Jack stood up.

"Thank goodness you're here, Mr. President," Jack said, as he crossed the room to shake Sutton's hand. "I was afraid I might have to take a crash course in French just to keep up here."

Sutton laughed. "My French isn't so great either."

"Jojo," Jack said, going over to stand next to her. "I'd like to introduce you to President Robert Sutton."

Both Jojo and Sutton beamed as they shook hands. "It's great to finally meet you in person, Jojo. I've heard a great deal about you. Your dad's a phenomenal guy, too. This one's not too bad either," Sutton said, nodding at Jack.

"President Sutton, I just wanted to thank you for the passport. The government confiscates the travel documents for all leaders and their families, which had left me feeling like there was no way I'd ever be able to go anywhere outside of China."

"That's certainly no way to feel," Sutton said. "But, you'll really have to thank Jack for that, not me. It was the only thing he wanted, so how could I refuse?"

Jojo reached out and touched Jack's forearm, looking up at him with fondness. "I know how fortunate I am. The last time he came back from a trip, he brought me a passport, a puppy, and an expensive bottle of my favorite drink. I think I'll keep him."

"He's just wild about you." Sutton smiled. "Now, before our evening gets underway, would you ladies mind if Jack and I went into the Red Room for a few minutes? It won't take long."

"Of course not," Jojo said.

"We'll just continue the conversation we were having," Cam said.

Jack followed Sutton next door to the aptly named Red Room, with its red walls and red-accented furniture. Jack paused to admire some of the many paintings on the wall, all housed in different styles of ornate gold frames.

Sutton sat down on the sofa and Jack sat in a wingback chair across from him.

"I know about the threat to you and Jojo. You'll be briefed tomorrow, but I wanted you to know that we're taking it very seriously and will do whatever we can."

Jack nodded. "That's reassuring; thank you."

"Is there anything I should know before the trade meeting tomorrow?"

"No, sir. I want to be fair to both sides, so we'll conduct things just how I did with President Wang."

Sutton rubbed his palms together, nodding slowly. "Fair enough," he said, a slow grin appearing. "So. When are you going to propose to that exceptional lady out there? Do you have a ring?"

"I do not."

"You probably haven't had much time to go ring shopping."

"That's true, but even if I did, I wouldn't know where to start. It seems like bad practice—guy goes out and buys ring without his girl there to supervise. I'm clueless about that stuff. The only idea I have would be something with a red diamond. Though I know they're expensive. But what diamond isn't?"

Sutton nodded. "See? You know more than you think. And I think I can help. I know someone in Australia who's connected with the Argyle Diamond Mine. I'll give him a call. And just putting this out there, but— the Rose Garden would be a great venue for your wedding."

They returned to the dining room, Jojo and Cam still busy conversing in French. The attendants started bringing food in—many different types of sushi, a seaweed salad, little bowls of miso soup.

"If you'd like something different, just let us know," Sutton said as they sat down at the table.

"This looks great." Jack helped himself to some toro sashimi, a few pieces of spicy salmon maki, and a yellowtail handroll. He poured some soy sauce into a little dish and mixed in some wasabi. "But, I must ask—is it true the president pays for food at the White House?"

"It is true," Sutton said. "Though taxpayers pay for official government functions." He grinned. "Which tonight is."

Everyone began to eat. Jack ate a good size piece of yellow pickled ginger to clean his palate then he deftly used his chopsticks to pick up a large piece of yellowtail, enjoying its delectable texture and mild flavor.

"Honey," Cam said to Sutton, "did you know Jojo is a sculptor? I was thinking I would take her to the Sculpture Garden tomorrow, and then maybe get a bite to eat at the Empress Lounge. While you and Jack are having your meeting."

"That sounds perfect," Sutton said. He looked at Jojo. "If you've never been to the National Gallery of Art, I bet you'll really enjoy it. And I heard you're moving in a new place in Beijing! That's exciting."

Jojo set down her chopsticks. "It is," she said. "It's safer there, and the boutique hotel we'll be living in is quite nice. Or, will be once a few things are modified."

Jack laughed. "A few?"

"Okay, okay, more than a few. Some of the changes are rather big, actually, but they're working on it now and should be done by the time we're back in China. I'm eager to see how it turns out."

"They'll probably have two or three crews working on it twenty-four hours a day," Jack said. "Usually, the family of party leaders live in Zhong-nanhai. But, I can't imagine they would let a foreigner boyfriend call it home under any circumstances."

"So, tell me, Jojo," Sutton said. "What was the reaction in China to what Jack said on TV?"

Jack looked at Jojo, though he wasn't entirely sure he wanted to hear her response.

"Well, *one* person for sure was certainly surprised," she said, "and not in a good way, though Jack and I have that sorted out now. For everyone else? People in China want change. And Jack laid out a refreshingly clear argument why change is necessary. He brought a sense of optimism that hasn't been felt in a long time, if ever. People are hoping positive pressure on the government will force it to act. If one voice could have an impact on people, others are realizing they can too."

"Actually, Jojo only just very recently learned the full details," Jack said. "We met up with Joshua in Beijing the night before we left and he filled her in on more of the details."

Jojo laughed. "Yes, see, prior to that, I fully believed that Jack had been a spy!"

"I could see that," Cam said. She raised her eyebrows at Jack. "You have that look about you."

"Well, I am most certainly *not* a spy," Jack said. "Also, that reminds me, Joshua said the president of Israel would like me to go visit. They seem quite happy with how everything went down."

Sutton nodded enthusiastically as he finished chewing. "That's putting it mildly," he said. "Israel is *very* happy—China has stopped buying oil from Iran. You and Jojo should absolutely make a visit—you won't regret it."

By the time everyone was done with dinner, no one had room left for the cake and coffee on hand for dessert, but Jack didn't mind; he felt perfectly satiated.

"Thank you so much for joining us for dinner," Sutton said. "I have a phone call I need to make, so you'll have to excuse me, but what a great evening. You're a lovely couple."

Cam walked the two of them out, linking arms with Jojo as they walked. Jack thought back to earlier that evening on their way over, how nervous Jojo had been, how happy he felt now seeing her ease.

Their phones were returned before they exited, and Jojo and Cam held each other's hands and kissed each other on both sides of the cheek.

"Jack," Cam said, "I'm so glad I finally got to meet you in person."

"It was a pleasure to meet you too. I hope we'll see each other again."

Cam grinned. "Oh, you will!"

They rode in the SUV back to the hotel, deciding to stop for drinks at the hotel's bar, before heading up to their rooms. They each ordered a Grey Goose martini with olives (no frozen grapes on hand), and they sat at a quiet corner table for two.

"So," Jack said. "I'd say you made quite an impression this evening. And you were nervous!" He held his drink up. "To you, Jojo, truly the most remarkable woman I have ever had the pleasure of knowing."

She smiled and lowered her eyes for a moment, then lifted her glass and gently clinked it with his. They both took a sip.

"Cam is just so wonderful," Jojo said. "She made me feel at ease right away. She was just so genuinely friendly, like you could tell she wasn't pretending."

"I'm so glad you guys hit it off, I bet you'll have a great day tomorrow. And it was pretty neat to hear you guys conversing in French. Not that I had a clue what you were saying. Sutton didn't, either."

"I like him, too."

"He is a good guy. He cares about doing what's right and he's not a wimp. I respect that."

They finished their drinks and then ordered two more to bring their room. Denis and Tom escorted them, and Jack told them they weren't planning to go anywhere else for the rest of the evening—it had been a busy enough night as it was.

But the night wasn't quite over yet, it would seem. Jack's iPhone rang and when he looked he saw that it was an incoming FaceTime call, from his brother, Paul. "It's my brother," he said, a note of surprise in his voice. "I'm going to pick it up."

He accepted the call and there was his brother's face on the screen, Jack's own face in a smaller rectangle in the upper righthand corner.

"Hey, Paul," he said. "Good to hear from you—it's been a while."

"Yeah, no shit!" Paul said. "So long, in fact, you've moved to another country and somehow gotten your face broadcast all over the national news? And here I always thought you were just some boring finance guy. Damn, Jack, what is up? Where are you?"

"I'm in DC, as a matter of fact. We're staying at the W."

"We?"

"I'm here with Jojo. Would you like to meet her?"

"Of course! The only info I know about her is what I've read online. Which is how I've been keeping up with you, too, and that just isn't right, now, is it Jack, considering we're brothers and all?"

"Let me introduce you to Jojo."

He walked over to her and held the phone so her face was now in the little rectangle in the corner.

"Hi Paul!" Jojo said. "So nice to finally meet someone from Jack's family!"

"Likewise!" Paul said. "Jack has always kept his social circle at an arm's distance from me, even when we were kids. I think he was afraid that his friends would like me more, because I'm the fun brother. But even the funnest of brothers couldn't top what he just did in China. Jesus Christ, Jack, what do you have to be a spy or something to pull a stunt like that off?"

Jack grimaced and pulled the phone back so he could look into the camera. "No, Paul, I'm not a spy and you know that. It's good to hear from you as always." He pressed the phone against his chest for a moment and looked at Jojo, gave her a chagrined smile, then held the phone back up.

"So, big bro, how long are you state-side for?"

"We haven't decided yet. We'd like to take some time and see some sights, but we have some meetings and other business to take care of here, first."

"Well, what about a little road trip to good old Sedona and visit your brother in person? You can stay at my place. I'll make you guys breakfast every morning."

Jack smiled, a memory of his brother trying to fry an egg on the pavement on a particularly hot summer day coming to mind.

"Is that so," he said. "That might be an offer too good to turn down. Let me talk to Jojo and I'll get back to you. Like I said, we have some business we have to take care of here, but after that, we'll have some time. Our place is being renovated right now in Beijing, so we certainly don't have to rush back there."

Paul frowned. "Beijing? I thought you lived in Shanghai."

"We're moving to Beijing. It's a long story though; maybe I'll tell you over breakfast."

"Guess that means you'll be coming to visit after all. Looking forward to it! Bye, Jojo!"

Jojo leaned over so Paul could see her face. "Bye, Paul! Great to meet you."

"I'll be in touch soon, Jack," Paul said. "Or you could just show up on my doorstep, I'm cool with that, too. Later!"

He disconnected the call before Jack had a chance to say goodbye, which was typical for his brother, who had always been the more impulsive, and yes, fun-loving, of the two.

"He seems nice," Jojo said. "I can see the resemblance." She reached up and brushed a few strands of hair back from Jack's forehead. "You're far more handsome, though."

He smiled, then leaned down and gave her a kiss. "Girls were always more interested in Paul when we were younger."

"Well, not this girl."

"I'm very happy to hear that," Jack said. He gave her another kiss, and then let Jojo lead him into the bedroom.

CHAPTER 6

The first meeting of the day was with Cooper, Davis, and a man named Rosenkranz.

"He's the point person in charge of your security, and this security matter in particular," Cooper said. Rosenkranz wore a crisp gray suit and a black tie that matched the thick head of black hair he had. He was about Jack's height and very fit, with intelligent blue eyes.

"Good to meet both of you," he said, shaking first Jack's hand, then Jojo's, before they all sat down at the conference table. "I'd like to get you up to speed with the current situation. We have confirmation from China that a man by the name of Zhang Zhong is the head of a group committed to retaliation for what Jack did in the CCTV Control Center." Rosenkranz paused, and Jack mulled the name over—He didn't recognize it. "He was closely aligned to many in former president Zhao Lihong's administration, and when Wang Yang took over, Zhang Zhong's assets were compromised. Chinese intel says he holds you, Jack, personally responsible, as well as Wang Yang, and his family," he added, looking now at Jojo. "He is a nationalist, a Maoist, and he believes he is acting in the interest of the nation. To put it simply: he's a fanatic."

Jack took a deep breath. Next to him, Jojo nodded, the expression on her face neutral. Jack wasn't so much afraid for himself as he was for Jojo's safety. Being Wang Yang's daughter did put her at a certain amount of risk, but he knew that being his girlfriend put her at even greater risk.

"Does Zhang Zhong have a nickname?" Jack asked, racking his brain. The name just wasn't ringing any bells. "Do you have any photos of him?"

There was a laptop on the table that Rosenkranz reached for and opened. He tapped a few keys and then slid it in front of Jack and Jojo. Jack recognized the man in the photo immediately.

"He is also known as Mr. Big," Rosenkranz said, eyeing Jack. "I take it from the look on your face that you know him."

"Yes, I know that shithead," Jack said. "I met him at the Roosevelt Club in Shanghai." The evening came roaring back to him with the clarity of a movie scene. Mr. Big's standoffish, pouty expression. His hostility and aggression. Jack clenched his jaw. This was not the sort of person he wanted out to get him. "Stanley Ling and Andrew San invited me there, back when I was first going to start working with them. And yeah, this guy is definitely a fanatic. I remember he demanded to know why I had sold THAAD to South Korea."

"How did you reply?" Cooper asked.

Jack shrugged. "It was a rude question; I almost considered not even acknowledging. But I could tell he was the sort of person who wouldn't let something like that go, so I told him that America gave South Korea THAAD to protect their country from North Korean missiles. I also reminded him that it was America who defeated Japan in World War Two, and if it weren't for America, Japan would have conquered China and he'd be speaking Japanese right now."

Rosenkranz shot a look at Cooper and then returned his gaze to Jack. "Well," he said. "Zhang Zhong has since gone underground. No one can find him or any of his close associates. There's only so much we can do since he's based in China, and we're relying on China for intel."

"Does he have assets in the United States or other countries?" Jack asked. They might have to rely on Chinese intel, but there were other things they could be doing, too. "What's going on with his money in China? Do you have a record of his Alipay and WePay expenditures? Have all his accounts been frozen? There must be some sort of trail; no one just completely disappears these days. Does he have kids studying abroad? A wife? Mistresses?"

Everyone looked to Rosenkranz, who had a decidedly embarrassed look on his face. He looked down before finally meeting Jack's gaze. "We're trying to look into that but haven't come up with anything."

Jack felt Jojo reach for his hand underneath the table. He gave it a gentle squeeze, trying to communicate to her that things were going to be all right, which was certainly harder now, because Jack really wasn't sure if they were going to be safe after all. "So you're telling me you have good information that this person, who is head of a group seeking revenge, has now just disappeared. And you have no idea where he is."

"Yes, but we are doing everything we can to find out his whereabouts."

"Not everything," Jack said witheringly. "Because if you had been doing *every*thing, you'd have more answers than what you're giving us."

Jack turned his attention to Cooper. "You cannot rely on China to do your job, which is to keep Jojo and me from being assassinated. I am disappointed in the lack of information in this briefing. All those questions I just asked should have been readily answered. Instead—crickets." He shook his head. "In light of this information—or lack thereof, should I say—I think Jojo and I will extend our stay here in the United States for a little while. We'll go to Los Angeles for a few days and then take a road trip to Sedona to see my brother. That should give everyone a little more time to try and come up with some better answers. I assume we'll be safer on U.S. soil than in China?"

"I think that's a safe assumption," Rosenkranz said.

Jack frowned. He took a deep breath and let it out slowly, then another, because if he did not, he was afraid he was going to end up saying something he didn't mean. "That's not an acceptable answer. I hereby formally give notice that this situation isn't being handled with the level of professionalism and urgency it requires."

He stood up, and Jojo followed. The other men in the room did as well, looking chastised. Jack felt a fleeting guilt, that he had been too hard, but that quickly dissipated because he knew he in fact had not.

As they left the room, Jojo gripped his arm. "That was intense," she whispered.

"I know. Not what I was expecting to hear at all. But I don't want you to worry. I will do whatever I can to make sure you are safe."

Jojo started to say something, but before she could, an armed guard approached.

"Ms. Wang," he said, "I'm here to escort you to the First Lady. Right this way, please."

"I'll see you back at the hotel," Jack said, dropping a kiss on her forehead. "Try to enjoy your day with Cam, okay? We'll talk about this later."

Jojo smiled up at him and gave him a quick kiss on the lips. "I will, thanks. And I hope your meeting goes better than this one did."

He watched until Jojo and the guard had disappeared around a corner.

"You were really professional in there," Davis said as he exited the room. He and Jack were alone in the hallway. "I know that wasn't what you wanted to hear."

Jack rubbed his hand over the lower part of his face. "You're right about that. I couldn't believe my ears, to be honest. They're essentially admitting they have no clue what's going on and have done next to nothing to try to get some answers about this guy."

"Well, you certainly gave them plenty of places to get started." If Jack wasn't mistaken, Davis was looking at him with a bit of admiration. "Come on, let's get you to that next meeting."

Jack followed Davis upstairs to the Cabinet Room, which was on the first floor near the Oval Office. They were a little early, so Jack took a seat at the conference table and pulled his laptop from his briefcase to review his notes. Davis asked if Jack needed anything.

"Some coffee would be great," Jack said.

"Sure. I'll go find someone to bring some in."

With the room to himself, Jack tried to focus on his notes and what they were going to talk about in the meeting, but his mind kept spinning back to Zhang Zhong, and the fact that no one seemed to have any idea where he was. How could they not be taking this more seriously? Why were they not tracking this man's every movements? And what about this group that Zhang Zhong was heading up? Surely someone within that circle had an idea where the man was.

He was so lost in thought he didn't even hear the woman enter the room, a cheerful young lady who had a cup of hot coffee for him. "I'm sorry to interrupt, Mr. Gold," she said, "but here's your coffee."

His focus snapped back to the present and he smiled, took the coffee. "Apologies," he said. "I have a lot on my mind. Thank you for bringing this."

"Not a problem. Enjoy."

He took a tentative sip, then another. As he set the cup down, three people—two men and a woman—entered the room. Jack stood up and introduced himself. He shook hands with the Secretary of State, Thomas Redding; Secretary of Commerce, Marshall Rockwell; and Wanda Tong, special advisor to the president.

Jack and the others stood up when Sutton walked into the room. "Good morning, Mr. President," he said, shaking his hand.

"Good morning, Jack."

Jack took his seat.

"So," Sutton said. "I spoke with President Wang Yang about the escalation of trade difficulties between our countries and we thought Jack might be able to assist, which is why he's here today. Jack, as I'm sure you all know, has a good relationship with China, and a very deep knowledge of the country. So—the right man for the job. Jack, you've already met with Wang about some of the ideas you have. Would you like to share those with us?"

"Certainly," Jack said. "I met with Wang and proposed a framework for conducting negotiations. The framework was devised to overcome the challenges that both countries are facing. These include preconceived notions, political interferences, and lack of understanding."

"Can you give me an example of what you mean by *lack of* understanding?" asked Rockwell, the Secretary of Commerce.

"Sure. If China subsidizes its steel companies and they export to America below cost, what happens?" Jack paused, though he wasn't really expecting any of them to give him an answer. "China then has more U.S. dollars, and we have inexpensive steel to build everything cheaper. America gains, even though everyone will focus on the workers who lost their jobs." He looked at each of the four people in the room. "Is China a currency manipulator?"

"Yes," Rockwell said, and the others nodded.

"And what do you want from them?"

"We want their currency to freely float," Wanda said.

"Okay," Jack said. "That might sound all well and good, but what will really happen then?" He only paused for a second this time, because he knew none of them would have the right answer. "If they freely float their currency, it is estimated the RMB will depreciate by up to thirty-five percent. That will make their products vastly cheaper and the American stock market will nosedive. Which could harm U.S. manufactures and thus Sutton's chances of reelection."

Wanda nodded slowly. "I don't have all the answers," she said with a smile, "and that's why you're here, Jack!"

"I don't have all the answers either," he said. "But I *do* know what many of the problems are. I proposed to Wang that he commit three people and that America would do the same. With me, they would work independently from the outside world. Any recommendations we unanimously agree upon would have a guarantee for adoption." Sutton had his elbows on the table, his fingers steepled

"Sounds good so far," he said.

"There are a few stipulations," Jack continued. "One—I get to remove one person at my discretion, from each side. Two—those selected cannot speak with outsiders about internal activities. Three —whatever we come up with must be binding, even if it requires presidential actions you don't like."

Rockwell raised an eyebrow. "Jack, you're not an expert in economics."

"You're right, I'm not, so I hope you pick some good economists." Out of the corner of his eye, Jack saw Sutton smile. "I will, however, need a liaison to arrange visits from various organizations, such as the Hoover Institution."

He reached for his briefcase and pulled out a folder with four pieces of paper that he handed out to each person. "I've written up the terms for you to review and then sign, just as I did for Wang."

"Do you think Wang will sign?" Sutton asked as he glanced over the paper.

"I think so," Jack said. "He trusts me. China doesn't want to do something that is going to harm China, but I think they're beginning to realize there is the potential here for something positive to happen, in a way there really hasn't ever been before. And if they do nothing, everything remains the same, which is not what they want. Or what anyone wants, really."

Sutton looked up from the paper, at his two cabinet members and his advisor. "We'll review and discuss, but it looks pretty good, Jack. Thank you for putting this together, and for all your effort on it so far."

"Of course," Jack said. "And sir, before I depart, may I have a quick word?"

He waited until the room had cleared out and he was alone with the president. "Jojo and I had our briefing this morning about the threat against us. I'm concerned. They're *just* relying on Beijing. I found the intelligence that they do have to be woefully inadequate."

Sutton frowned. "That's not what I want to hear; it doesn't sound like it's being handled correctly at all. Let me look into it. The last thing you need, though, is to be worried that we aren't doing our job protecting you. Or Jojo. But I give you my word, Jack, I will personally look into it."

"Thank you."

"I don't want Jojo to be worried, either. Oh, I'm sure she and Cam are out having a wonderful day, probably speaking French the entire time. Well, good for them. Have you given any more thought about ring shopping?"

"Not yet."

"Well, you should."

Sutton stood and Jack followed suit, the two men exiting the Cabinet Room. Jack bid Sutton farewell and made his way toward the exit, where Cooper was waiting.

"Jack," he said. "About that back there, earlier . . . that wasn't in our hands, it's in the FBI's hands."

"I understand," Jack said. "And I'm not blaming you. But you understand my concern, I'm sure."

"I do."

"And I did mention something to the president about it, and he's going to look into it. That's all I can do, I guess, except keep checking over my shoulder."

Cooper grimaced. "You're not going to have to handle this on your own, Jack. Contrary to the way it might have come across."

"I haven't completely lost faith yet," Jack said, cracking a smile. He didn't want Cooper to feel guilty over it, as the matter was out of his control.

"So, you want to go to LA and then on to Sedona?"

"Yeah. I can show Jojo the west coast and where I grew up and then we can drive over to Sedona. Maybe we'll stop in Vegas first and *then* head on to Sedona so she can meet my brother."

"That sounds like a plan. Do you know where you'd like to stay?"

"I was thinking Shutters on the Beach, in Santa Monica."

"Ah, good choice. What about in Vegas? Have you been to the Cosmopolitan? I know the place. You guys would love it there. Let me know and I can make arrangements."

"I read about the Cosmopolitan. Two nights there sounds great. Jojo will love it. Thanks, Cooper, I appreciate the recommendation. Take care."

Jack retrieved his phones on the way out and hurried over to Davis's SUV. Davis asked how he was doing, to which Jack replied *Good*, but he didn't elaborate about much and instead said he wanted to go back to the hotel.

"Sure thing," Davis replied.

Jack stared out the window as they drove, but he didn't notice anything, the buildings going by in a blur. Jojo was out there, and he hated not being near her, though he also knew she was more than safe with Cam.

It was a relief to be back in his room, the door shut. He changed into more comfortable clothing and then lay back on the bed and shut his eyes, telling himself he'd rest for just a few minutes.

*   *   *

He awoke some time later, his arm being gently jostled, Jojo calling his name. When he opened his eyes, he smiled, because there she was, a happy, exhilarated look on her face.

"Sorry," he said, yawning as he sat up. "I must've fallen asleep. I was just going to rest my eyes for a few minutes."

"Well, if you fell asleep, you needed it."

"And what about you? It looks like you had a good day."

"I had an excellent day! Cam and I went to the Sculpture Garden—I was so impressed by the diversity of sculpture styles." She stood up, using one hand to brush back the hair from her face. Jack leaned against one of the pillows while she continued to talk. "Then, we went to the Empress Lounge at the Mandarin Hotel. The food there was better than anything I've had in France."

"It sounds like a great day; I'm so happy for you. And you and Cam got along! See, you had nothing to be worried about, I knew she would love you. How could she not?"

Jojo nodded. "You're right. And, I have to admit—I read an article about her some time back, and it was completely incorrect in the way it portrayed her. She's charming and funny. She has her own style and likes to do things her way."

Jack smiled. "Sounds just like someone else I know."

"What about your day? How was your other meeting?"

"It was fine. I also talked to Sutton about looking into stepping up the security efforts. I'll be honest—I don't like knowing this Zhang Zhong character is out for revenge. I'm not worried about my safety so much as your own. You know I would never be able to forgive myself if something happened to you."

"Your concern is touching. But I am a big girl, too, you know."

"Of course I know that. This guy though . . . He's bad news. I didn't get a good vibe when I first met him, and I'm sure as hell not thinking any more highly of him knowing what I know now." He waved a hand. "But,

I'd also say we're relatively safe here in the US. So what do you think about going to LA and spending a few days there? We can see how we feel, maybe stop in Las Vegas on the way to see my brother?"

Jojo was nodding before Jack had even finished. "I love it," she said. "I want to see as much as possible. And I've never been to Las Vegas before, but I've heard about it."

"I'll let Paul know. He'll be psyched."

And Jack was looking forward to it, too, not just getting to see his brother, but also the chance to return to LA, to show Jojo a little bit of his childhood, and then, to Vegas. He knew she had never been there and could find it fascinating.

CHAPTER 7

The hotel was right on the beach, and their suite had a magnificent view of sand silk beaches, grandly waving palms, the sunlight glittering like diamonds off its textured surface. The first day they just relaxed, first on the beach, and then in their suite after they'd gone out to eat. The next day, they rented a car to drive up the coast. "I feel like I could be in a movie," Jojo said as she got into the bright yellow Mustang hardtop.

"Traveling in style," Jack said. He made his way to Ocean Blvd. and then onto the Pacific Coast Highway, which ran parallel to the beach. Then he angled up to Corona Del Mar. He could see, in the rearview mirror, Tom and Denis a few car lengths behind him in their black SUV.

"This is the street I grew up on," he said.

"It's beautiful."

Jack looked, tried to see it as an outsider, as someone who hadn't lived here and didn't have all the memories associated with it. It was beautiful, yes, with the palm trees, the Spanish-style houses with their terra cotta roofs, and everyone's favorite neighbor, the beach, right there.

"It is," he agreed, "but it's also deceiving. The house I grew up in was too big."

"Too big?"

"I know, it sounds stupid. But it's true—we never really saw much of each other, because there was so much space everyone could kind of retreat and do their own thing. Which isn't always bad, but it's also not good if that's what happens all the time."

He thought back to his childhood, when it was mostly him and Paul, left to their own devices to find their own fun. Not a bad way to grow up, though Jack always felt like his little brother's de facto babysitter—their mom busy in her art studio, their father with his medical practice. Paul always wanting to do something that had the potential to get them in trouble—ride bikes on the golf course, sneak into the country club's exclusive pool, "borrow" their father's car at night and go meet up with girls. It was always Paul who seemed to come up with the plans, and it was always Jack who was expected to either go along with it or talk his little brother out of it. Though he was older, Jack had always felt a little bit like he'd been living in his brother's shadow, if for no other reason than he was the better behaved one.

They stopped at the Palisades Farmers Market, which occupied a two-lane street under a canopy of large shade trees. Shops lined both sides of the streets—restaurants, clothing stores, an ice cream store that boasted thirty-one different flavors. The food stalls were concentrated in one area, offering only the best of local produce for this affluent neighborhood. There was a strict policy that only the actual growers could sell their fruit and vegetables. They bought two quarts of organic strawberries, as red as rubies.

For lunch, Jack drove Jojo to Beverly Hills to the renowned delicatessen, Nate n' Al's, one of his favorite places. The place was crowded, though, and they were told there was a half hour wait.

"Why don't we walk around while we wait," Jack said. They headed toward Rodeo Drive, the famous street, home to many high-end brands. There was a specific place Jack had in mind though, and he led Jojo past the two guards, into Cartier.

Jojo gave him a quizzical look when she realized what the store was, a look that deepened when Jack asked one of the employees there if Jojo could get her ring finger measured.

"Just for my own personal knowledge," he said.

"Fifteen point two millimeters," the woman told him. "A four-and-a-half in U.S. sizes."

"Thank you," Jack said. "That's exactly what I needed to know."

"What was that all about?" Jojo asked, once they had left the store and were walking down the sidewalk, arm in arm. There were crowds of people everywhere, almost everyone beautiful, immaculately dressed. There were tourists, busy taking selfies and gawking at the high-end shops, the luxury sports cars.

"Just to satisfy my curiosity," Jack said.

Jojo pursed her lips, and slowly smiled. "I think I like the idea where this is headed."

He gave her an innocent, wide-eyed look. "Why, whatever are you talking about?"

They arrived back to Nate'n Al's right as their name was being called. The crowd had thinned out a bit, and they were seated at a small booth; Denis and Tom were given seats a few tables away. Jojo ordered Eggs Benedict; Jack ordered the pastrami sandwich on toasted rye and a cup of matzo ball soup. They both requested coffee and water.

While they waited for the food, Jojo looked around. "The diversity here is extraordinary," she said. "I mean, not just in this restaurant, but everywhere we've been. Where are they all from?"

Jack smiled. "All over."

"It just makes me realize what a lack of diversity there is in China. And Shanghai, too." She frowned. "Which is strange, because Shanghai is supposed to be this international city. But now after being here, and seeing all the different cultures, and different people, it really doesn't seem that way at all. Why is that?"

Jack glanced to his right. There was a larger, six-person table booth next to them, separated only by a low dividing wall. The table was occupied by three middle-aged Chinese men, who were talking quietly amongst themselves, but every so often would glance at Jojo. He stared at one of the guys until he made eye contact with Jack, and Jack continued to look at him until he looked away.

"I think there are three reasons," he said, his attention turning back to Jojo. "First, very few foreigners speak Chinese well, so companies don't want them. Second, China makes it difficult to get visas, making it virtually impossible for people from other countries to live there. And, third, most feel that China doesn't want to be some great melting pot like America—China wants its own citizens and country, and that's it."

Jojo frowned. It probably wasn't the answer she wanted to hear, but it was the truth.

When their food arrived, they set aside all talk of China and instead focused on enjoying the feast in front of them.

"I can say with certainty that is the biggest sandwich I've ever seen," Jojo said, eyeing Jack's plate. He grinned and pushed it toward her.

"Here, have a bite."

He watched as she tried to navigate the sandwich, which was a good four or five inches thick, layers of pastrami with cole slaw and Russian dressing, sandwiched between two slices of toasted rye. She compressed the sandwich the best she could and managed to get a decent-sized bite from one of the corners. She closed her eyes as she chewed, and Jack waited until she was finished and her eyes had reopened, to ask her how it was.

"This is quite easily the best sandwich I've ever had. Wow." She looked at her own plate of Eggs Benedict. "I'm not sure how that is going to be able to compare to this."

"Why don't you eat that half, I'll take this one," Jack said. He hadn't come here to eat Eggs Benedict, after all. "If we're still hungry after this and the soup, we'll split yours."

"Deal," Jojo said, squeezing the sandwich together again as she prepared to take another bite.

"By the way, Cooper is helping us with accommodations in Las Vegas. I figure we'd regret not stopping by since it's on the way to Sedona."

"I've only seen Las Vegas in the movies. If you think it'll be fun, let's do it."

"Okay, there is a new hotel there I checked out called The Cosmopolitan that sounds pretty good. We can maybe spend two nights there and relax, maybe see a show. It's about a five-hour drive."

"I'm all in."

Jack grinned. "Now that sounds like a gambling term. Have you ever played blackjack before?"

"Never."

"Now we have to go!" Jack took out his phone and sent a text to Cooper to confirm.

He put the phone away and turned his focus to the meal. Yet while they ate, Jack couldn't help but notice the way the three men kept glancing over at them. They were speaking in Chinese, but in a dialect he couldn't understand, and even if he could, it seemed every time one of them said something, they leaned their heads together so it would have been impossible for Jack to make out what they were saying. He looked over at Tom and Denis, who did not appear to think anything was amiss. Maybe he was being paranoid.

"Everything okay?" Jojo asked. They had just finished the Eggs Benedict, the two plates completely clear in front of them.

"Yeah," Jack said, glancing at the three guys. It was probably nothing, just some guys being creeps and checking out his girlfriend. He signaled the waitress for the check. The sooner they could get out of there, the better.

*   *   *

Early the next morning they exited the hotel. Waiting out front for them was a hard-top Mustang, which Davis was standing next to. Beyond him, Jack could see the beach, the sun shining down on the water.

"Good morning," Davis said as they made their way over to the car. "I guessed you wouldn't mind the Mustang."

"Davis, you chose perfectly. Thank you. Beautiful day for a drive."

"We'll be there along with you. Any plans to stop along the way?"

"I was thinking we might stop just outside of Vegas at the Denny's there. It's the last place for breakfast before arriving into town."

Davis waved, "Sounds good, have a fun drive."

They got in and Jack put the car into gear and pulled out without any hesitation. He felt comfortable. Diving to Vegas was piece of cake, something he had done many times before. Except now, he had Jojo at this side, as well as a security detail.

They kept the windows partially down and Jojo tied her hair back to keep it from blowing around her face. It truly was a perfect day for a drive: blue skies, bright sun, warm but not uncomfortable. Most of the traffic was going the other direction so Jack kept his foot solidly on the accelerator. They made their way onto Highway 15 where there was even less traffic. Jack turned on the radio to an 80s music station. Jojo grinned and turned the volume up, dancing along in her seat.

"I don't know most of these songs," she said, "but I love them!"

Jack put his window down further and let his arm hang out, the air rushing through his fingers. He took a deep breath, enjoying the clean, pure air, such a contrast from Beijing or Shanghai. All around them were vast expanses of open space, the highway unfurled before them, seemingly all the way to the horizon.

"Eye of the Tiger" came on: *Rising up, back on the street. Did my time, took my chances. Went the distance, now I'm back on my feet. Just a man and his will to survive.* Jack smiled; a perfect anthem for everything he'd been through recently, and now, here he was, having gone the distance and was back on his feet, headed to Las Vegas with his lady.

The two SUVs kept up with them easily. Jojo had her iPhone out and was taking pictures of the clouds, the view of the road, the cactuses.

"These cactuses are so interesting," she said as she snapped pictures. "I've never seen them in real life before."

When they arrived in the town of Baker, Jojo saw a store and pointed to the sign. "What's that, 'Alien Jerky'?" she asked.

Jack enjoyed seeing Jojo experiencing this part of America for the first time and the expressions it brought to her face. "Just a cool beef jerky place. Wanna stop and get some?" He could only imagine what she thought it might look like inside since most beef jerky in China was sold in outdoor food stalls.

"No. It's okay. Great name for beef jerky, though. Alien, *wàixīngrén.*"

They decided to eat at the hotel in Vegas and pass Denny's. It was still early and Jack thought chances were good they could find something better.

Jojo's eyes lit up as they pulled onto the Vegas Strip. She lifted up her camera again and started filming the buildings and then the fountain in front of the Bellagio Hotel. Jack turned down the music, smiling for the video when Jojo turned the phone toward him, his hair flying from the wind. "Vegas baby!" he said, grinning.

"Show off. This place is massive. I had no idea. Look at all the people on the streets walking around! And, there is the Eiffel Tower! Wow. It looks identical to the real one. We have to take a picture with it."

"See the Bellagio." Jack said, pointing. "It's a famous hotel right behind the fountains. We can walk by tonight and see the light and water show. That's our hotel, The Cosmopolitan, right next to it. I'll pull in up here and let the valet do the parking."

Inside the hotel lobby, they saw about eight crowded counters to check in and over a hundred people waiting in line. Instead, Jack opted to enter the "Member" entrance to see if he could get some special assistance.

There was a young woman with dyed black hair behind the counter, which was much less busy than the others they'd just seen. She smiled at him. "Hello, welcome to The Cosmopolitan."

"Hi, we'd like to check in. We're a little early."

Her smile didn't waver. "That's not a problem at all. Let's see what we can do for you. May I have your name?"

"Sure, Jack Gold."

She tapped some of the keys on the keyboard, squinted at the screen for a moment. "Ah. I see you right here. May I see your ID please? We've booked you in a nice suite overlooking the fountain."

Jack gave her his passport, which she looked at and then returned. Then she handed both him and Jojo keys. "Here you go. You're on the thirty-ninth floor. Everything is taken care of."

Jack hesitated. "That's it? You don't need a credit card?"

"No need," the woman said, waving him off. "You are all taken care of. We always comp rooms to high rollers. That must be you. Enjoy your stay."

"What was that all about?" Jojo asked as they made their way to the elevators. "We're high rollers?"

"I guess so." Jack glanced at the lobby as they passed, the counter lines which looked like they had barely moved. "At least we're not still standing in line."

The suite was perfect, two rooms with nicely appointed furniture, clean lines, and a good view of the fountain. Jack went into the bedroom and stretched out on the king size bed. "The bed is comfortable," he said. "Are you hungry?"

Jojo came into the bedroom and lay down next to him. "Oooh, this is comfortable. And yeah, let's eat something."

Jack sat up and reached down to get his iPad out of his bag he'd placed next to the bed. "Let me check their website and see what restaurants they have."

He fluffed up the pillow and settled back onto the bed, Jojo curling up next to him as he typed in "Cosmopolitan." Lots of pictures of cool people appeared. He then went to the top navigation bar pulling it down and saw something interesting: "Exclusive Reads, Beauty & Style, and Sex & Relationship." Jack looked down at Jojo then selected "Sex & Relationships."

The page opened to a black and white photo of a couple kissing. He scrolled down further and saw some soft porn cartoons of people having sex, with the caption "sex positions to bookmark for later ;)."

"Why is this hotel recommending sex positions?" Jojo asked. "What kind of place have you brought me to?"

"Errr . . ." Jack laughed. "I think we're on the wrong site. This hotel shares a name with a women's magazine. I'll find the right site."

"Well, hold on now," Jojo said. She gave him a sly smile. "We might be able to learn something. Start scrolling!" Jack did as she requested, scrolling through so they could see all the positions.

"You'll have to bookmark this for later," Jojo said. "That's a lot of positions!"

"You have a one-track mind," Jack said. "All right, let's find the right website."

There were numerous choices, but they decided the second floor would be best to explore since it had a bunch of places to get a quick bite.

"We'll just stroll around and see what looks good," Jack said.

They settled on Hattie B's Hot Chicken and a salad and took it up to their room and devoured it.

*   *   *

At sunset, they walked over to Caesars Palace and the Bellagio to see the shops, the casinos, and people watch. Jojo had her phone out, taking photos, filming short clips. There were crowds of people, from all walks of life, the buildings lit up in a kaleidoscope of colors, giving everything the circus atmosphere that Vegas was renowned for. Huge digital billboards showed faces of well-known singers and entertainers, broadcasting the date and time of their next performance. A group of Elvis impersonators walked by. A light breeze ruffled the palm fronds that lined the strip.

They stopped and watched the water fountain show that was already in progress. She took a few pictures of Jack in front of the fountain and then passed her phone to him.

"Here, now take a picture of me in front of the fountain."

Jack obliged and let some people pass before he quickly snapped several pictures of her from different angles, as she changed her pose, making silly faces. She was a grown woman but she still knew how to let her inner child out, and Jack loved it.

They walked around a little more and then decided to return to the hotel. "How about a drink, on the way back to the room?" Jack asked.

"You read my mind."

They found two seats next to each other at the bar in the casino. Jojo turned on her seat to watch the people as they milled about, played the slot machines, sat hunched at the tables, playing craps and Texas Hold 'Em.

She turned back around, facing the bar, and leaned toward Jack. "Everyone is fat," she said in Chinese.

Jack raised an eyebrow. "Not everyone!"

As if on cue, the bartender came over, a middle-aged, overweight man. "What can I get you to drink?"

Jojo shrugged and looked at Jack. "What should I get? Order something for me. Surprise me."

"Gladly," Jack said. He looked at the bartender. "The lady would like to have your best Cosmopolitan and I'll have a Heineken."

"Certainly. Coming right up."

"What's in a Cosmopolitan?" Jojo asked.

"I don't recall what's in it, but I'm guessing it's pretty much the perfect drink for you right now. Everyone in *Sex and the City* drinks one, and it shares the name with this hotel, so I figure that's good enough."

The drinks were mixed and put in front of them. Jojo's Cosmopoliton was in a martini glass; the drink was watermelon pink with a twist of lemon on the rim. She took a tiny sip. Her eyes lit up at the taste and she took a bigger sip.

"Wow," she said. "Now that is *good.*"

Jack took a sip of his Heineken. "I thought you'd like it."

Jojo took another sip and then set her glass down. "What's this?" she asked, motioning to a screen that was embedded into the bar.

"That," Jack said, "is electronic poker and blackjack. Ever played?"

"I have not."

"Well, let's give it a try, then." He took a twenty from his wallet and fed it into the machine. "We'll do blackjack," he said, pressing the button for that game. "Let me show you how to play. It's all about probability. Try to get as close to twenty-one as possible, or under." Jojo watched him play a few rounds.

"Okay, let me play." Jojo elbowed him out of the way after taking another generous sip of her drink.

Jojo was fascinated with the game and, Jack thought, to her credit she had learned quickly. He had not had to add any money, with her balance briefly going above and below twenty dollars. Two drinks later he said, "How about we walk around the casino and check things out? Looks like everything is filling up and coming alive."

"What do I do now? How do I get my money back?"

Jack leaned forward, "You press this button and a ticket will come out. Then, we need to go to a cashier to get the cash."

"That's stupid. Why don't they just use WeChat and you can scan a code and the money goes directly to your bank account?"

"I agree," Jack said. "I wish WeChat were used throughout American."

Jojo collected the ticket and after paying their bill, minus two free drinks, made their way casually over to the cashier.

Walking through the casino back to their room Jojo saw lots of older people playing the slot machines. They also saw some tables packed with young people enthusiastically yelling. And, they saw others, those who had lost money, those in private high-roller rooms, those who were about to get married, those dressed in tuxedos, those in shorts. Jack saw Jojo seeing another slice of America. Most of the people and scenes were completely different from anything she had seen in China. It was a melting pot of all sorts of people, with different personalities, different skin colors, different socioeconomic status.

Upstairs, the fountain had started again. They enjoyed the view from a new angle from their balcony, Jojo filming away. "You can even hear the fountain here!" she marveled.

They sat on the outside sofa and enjoyed the sight while Jojo used her phone to put together a video with music to post to her WeChat profile. "There. Done. You should check it out," she said.

He did. She had posted a video with "Viva Las Vegas" as the soundtrack, using the film clips and photos she'd taken so far to highlight their trip. "This is great," Jack said.

Jojo looked down, "Fifty of my friends already pressed *Like*."

Jack was amazed. That was so many people responded so fast. That's how people kept others up-to-date on what they were doing, like America's Facebook but so much better.

"How did I get so lucky to end up with such a talented girlfriend?" he asked.

Jojo grinned, her face still a little flushed from the drinks. "Let's go see if we can remember a few of those positions from the *other* Cosmopolitan website."

He handed her the phone back and stood up, following her into the suite. "You lead the way."

*   *   *

They got up leisurely the next morning, went down to the hotel buffet. "Did you have anything in mind you wanted to do today?" Jack asked. He felt relaxed, more relaxed than he had felt in a while, and he relished this whole day ahead of them, in a different place, where they could really do whatever they felt like. It was the first time in a while where his mind was thoroughly sidetracked from China and anything he had to do. This was a vacation, after all. "There are lots of great shows," he said to Jojo over his plate of eggs, bacon, and hash browns, as well as all the hot black coffee he could drink. "I'm sure there's some good ones. Anyway interest?"

Jojo was stirring granola into yogurt. "What else can we do?"

"It's Vegas. We can go skydiving, helicopter riding, go-karting, see a rock star, anything you want. But there are some great singers here, and the other shows, like The Blue Man Group, are great."

"I don't know," Jojo said, looking less enthused about the prospect of a show than Jack was expecting. "I really love the freedom of moving around. I don't feel like sticking to a schedule at all. Like, we'd have to buy tickets for the show and then we'd have to be there at a specific time. That all sounds pretty unappealing."

"Fair enough," Jack said. He was even willing to concede that he did, in a way, feel similar. Not having anywhere to go, no specific time to be somewhere—that was the true freedom of a vacation. "We'll do it how you're suggesting," he said. "No itinerary, we'll just see what comes up. Though there are so many great restaurants. Maybe the best in the world?"

Jojo wrinkled her nose. "You know our definition of a good restaurant is different from anyone else's."

Jack knew she was right; they were spoiled by all the food in China. "How about after this then, we go relax by the pool?"

Now she looked enthusiastic. "We can watch people from the pool. That sounds great."

The pool was located on the second floor, where lithe women in bikinis and well-muscled men with tans relaxed on lounge chairs. There were also some families with kids challenging each other to see who could do the best cannonball, the straightest pencil dive. The drinks were flowing and there were a few empty chairs that Jack and Jojo walked over to. Jack had brought his iPad to read an ebook; Jojo was focused on her phone, replying to all the people who asked where she was and what was she doing. He stopped reading and gazed at her as she typed something back on her phone, a smile on her face, which he was happy to see. She, too, was having fun. They had needed time to themselves more than he realized.

After relaxing for a few hours, Jojo asked if they should go for a swim.

Jack put his iPad down. "See all those kids over there? See the water? They've been peeing in it all day."

"That's gross. How about we go take a shower, then?"

"That's probably the best thing someone can do in Vegas."

*   *   *

That evening for dinner they went to Beijing Noodle No. 9. Jack had thought he might bring Jojo to Gordon Ramsay's Hell's Kitchen, but when he mentioned the noodle place, she had practically started salivating.

"Do they really have a Beijing noodle place?"

"Yes, they do."

She stopped putting on her lipstick and caught Jack's eye in her reflection in the mirror. "I'm dying for some Chinese food. Noodles sounds great."

As they walked over to the nearby Caesars Palace, they went through the same path as the previous night. Rounding the corner they could see a short line of Chinese outside of the restaurant's entrance. They were not the only ones craving Chinese food.

After they ordered, Jack looked through the crowd, trying to get a sense of whether the Chinese were visiting from China, or lived in America. It really didn't matter. He turned his attention back to Jojo. She was looking at the nearby tables to see the food, eager to eat. They could readily see that the restaurant was not luxurious as many Vegas places. It was focused on the food instead. Chinese did not care what a restaurant looked like, as long as the food was good.

When their food arrived, Jojo eagerly tried her noodle soup with spinach and watercress. Jack waited to try his. "How it is?"

"It's passable. Not the best I've had, but it's what I needed."

Jack took a bite of his noodle soup, with beef and chicken. "Agreed. The Chinese food in American never seems as good as that in China."

But, he was glad to see that Jojo ate all of it, and seemed satisfied. When they were done eating, Jojo wanted to go back to the bar and play some more Blackjack.

"Sure," Jack said. "That'd be fun."

They paid the bill and headed over, observing the fountain as they passed by it but not stopping to watch the show this time. The bar was busy like last time, but they were able to find two seats next to each other.

"Would you like another Cosmopolitan?" Jack asked.

"I think those delicious drinks gave me a good luck, So, yes."

Jack ordered for them and Jojo started to play, inserting her own twenty-dollar bill, a deeply focused expression on her face.

She was in the zone, Jack could tell, and she wasn't going to be looking to him for any stimulating conversation. So he took out his own twenty and put it into the machine in front of him. He was aware of Jojo out of the corner of his eye, tapping the screen, brow furrowing, a smile appearing, then disappearing, then coming back, slightly. She was in her own separate world. Jack wondered what sort of casinos they'd have in the metaverse–they'd probably be able to virtually walk into any number of casinos by simply putting on a pair of goggles. It was simply a matter of time. Vegas was unreal enough.

They played for a while, neither really winning or losing. Jack looked to the bartender and closed out the tab.

"I hate to interrupt a good time," he said, "but it's time to go and play for real."

She finally looked up at him. "What are you talking about?"

"You can't just play an electronic game; we're going to play some real life games. At the tables. You'll have to bet more, though."

Jojo took her receipt, "How much is the bet at the tables?"

"Minimum is twenty-five per hand."

"That's too much. We can play here a long time just on twenty dollars."

"Let's pretend it's just tokens and for fun. The key is to find a good table."

She did not look quite convinced but Jack knew she'd love it once she sat down. They got up and began to walk around the casino, looking for a Blackjack table. He discreetly pointed to a table with an older man leaning against his elbow looking exhausted, like he had just lost his life's savings. "How about that one?"

Jojo looked, saw the man, and shook her head. "No."

Another table had some rowdy young kids around it with one free seat. They kept walking around the floor, passing tables that were unsuitable, including some that had a minimum bet of fifty dollars.

They had almost reached the end of the room when they spotted a couple occupying one side of a table. Jack and Jojo looked at each other and decided to take a seat.

When the hand was done, Jack handed the dealer $1,000 and received some chips in return, placing half in front of Jojo.

"I thought you said it was twenty-five dollars," she hissed.

"Pretend they are chips, not money, and remember—we are here just to have fun."

The couple lend forward, "Is this your first time playing Blackjack?" the woman asked. Both she and the man were middle-aged, slightly overweight; he was balding, she had short, dyed blond hair.

"It is," Jojo said. "I'm not sure what to do with all these chips!"

"Don't worry," the woman said in a voice with a Midwestern twang. "It'll be easy. Even the dealer will tell you what you should do if you ask." She smiled broadly at Jojo. "Where are you from, honey? Japan? I have a co-worker who hosted an exchange student from Japan once. Lovely young woman."

Jojo looked up from her pile of chips. "I'm from China."

"We had some great Chinese food last night," the man said.

"Was it at Beijing Noodle House No. 9?" Jojo said. "'Cause that's where we went."

The man's face lit up and he nudged his wife with his elbow. "Hey did you hear that? We went to that same place! Yeah, that place is great. Now, tell me, how does it compare to authentic? Because I thought it was pretty good, even if it was on the spicy side."

The woman rolled her eyes. "Harold, you can't handle spice at all. You think ketchup is spicy."

Jack suppressed a smile; Jojo was too distracted by the pile of chips, sitting at the table, to take offense to the benign racism that was typical from the average American. He bet twenty-five dollars, placing it in front of him. Jojo followed. The dealer dealt the two cards; Jojo got two tens. She knew what to do—nothing.

The dealer had a six showing and everyone on the table held pat all winning when the dealer took a card and broke twenty-one.

The hands continued. Occasionally Jojo bet two chips. And, when she got an eight and a three, she knew to double down. Roughly twenty-five minutes had passed. The dealer stepped back and a new dealer started to take over the deck.

Jack leaned to Jojo, looking at both of their piles of chips, which had grown markedly, "They are changing the dealer. Let's take what we have and run."

"We can just . . . leave?" she asked.

"Absolutely."

"Then let's go!" she said, grinning.

They picked up all their chips and thanked the people next to them.

"You're leaving so soon?" the woman asked. "But the night is still young! Look how well you're doing!"

Jack sympathized a little bit with them; they took gambling seriously and would likely spend entire the night in the casino. "Got to take our winnings while we have them!" They bid the couple goodbye and went to the cashier and traded their chips for cash.

"How much did you win?" Jack asked.

"Four hundred seventy-five!" She looked thrilled. "You?"

"Four twenty-five.. You got me beat. No one walks away from the tables when they are winning. We did good. What should we do with our winnings?"

"I can't believe it! That was so much fun. I even won more than you. What do I want to do with my winnings? Hmm." She furrowed her brow as she looked up at him. "I want to go to that little market on the second floor and buy some treats for us!"

"Sounds good. I'll buy us a few more drinks before we go up. Another Cosmopolitan?"

"Yes! I want you to have some tequila and another beer or two. You haven't been drinking at all. I'll buy that too!"

Jojo had her phone out, was looking at the photo she had taken of her receipt before she had given it to the cashier. "I'm sharing this on WeChat," she said. "With the caption *Se magnificent!*"

"I'm realizing what an excellent promoter you are," Jack said. "The city should put you on the payroll."

"What do you mean? I'm just sharing pictures."

"Yeah, but how many Chinese are going to see what you've been posting and not think that they too can come to Vegas and have as much fun as you are? Who knows how far your posts will reach."

"That's a good point, but they're not traveling with you, so obviously they won't be able to have nearly as much fun as me. I really am having such a great time though, I'm so glad we decided to come here."

"Well, we did it the right way: we didn't have to pay for the room and we made money at the tables. Trust me—that never happens."

"I just love the way you can do whatever you want. And there's so much diversity and so many interesting things to look at! And the gambling. I can see why some people spend their entire life's savings on it, it's a rush!"

The excitement of the win stayed with Jojo for the rest of the evening. It was gratifying to hear that she was having such a good time, and Jack was glad he got to be a part of it.

CHAPTER 8

Davis met them in the lobby. Jack guessed that they had spoken with the building security and were watching all the cameras including those in the elevators.

"Good morning. Congratulations on winning last night, to the both of you."

"Yes, Jojo has turned into a professional Blackjack player now."

"I won more than Jack!"

Davis turned to Jack "Which way are you going to go today?" he asked.

"Route 40," Jack said. "More scenic. I think Jojo will like that."

Davis nodded. "Okay. We'll be following close by."

"Great. Thank you."

Jack felt reassured, knowing that Davis and Tom and Denis would be nearby. He was eager to get going. The inside of the hotel was starting to weigh on him.

He took Highway 15 to Route 40, let his foot get a little heavy on the accelerator, this stretch of road was perfect for that. Next to him, Jojo stretched out and ate some strawberries, gazed out the window.

"It's so beautiful," she said. "The colors everywhere seem so vibrant. I don't know if I'd ever want to leave if I grew up here."

"It's not a bad place," Jack said. "And I used to wonder that myself sometimes—what would my life look like if I had just stayed here? Obviously, I'm glad I didn't, because I wouldn't have met you."

"Awww." Jojo touched his arm and gave him a smile. "You're so sweet. So. Are you excited to see your brother?"

"I am. It's been a while, and our life trajectories are totally different, but it'll be good to see him. And Sedona is beautiful."

Jojo took a bite of another strawberry she bought from the shop last night with her winnings. "You know," she said, chewing, "if you had told me a year ago that I'd be in the United States, driving toward the desert with my American boyfriend who played an integral role in helping my father become president, I would have asked you to share some of whatever you'd been smoking." She laughed. "But I really couldn't be happier."

Jack reached over and rest his hand on her leg. The scenery sped by, the sky a deep endless blue above them. He agreed with every word of her sentiment—sometimes, he couldn't believe it either, but also, in this moment, couldn't be happier.

*   *   *

After driving for several hours, they decided to stop off in Needles to get something to eat. It was close to one o'clock, and they'd made good time, with only about another hour or so to go. He took the exit ramp and drove underneath the freeway they'd just been on. The first places he saw were Desert Mirage Inn, Porky's BBQ, and River City Pizza Co. None looked too appealing, so he decided to drive a little further.

They stopped at a red light. A black Mercedes with tinted windows pulled up next to them.

It happened so fast. The windows on the right-hand side of the Mercedes rolled down. He saw the arms, the guns, and his subconscious kicked in before his mind had time to register what was actually happening. He stomped on the accelerator and yanked the wheel to the right as a spray of bullets hit their car.

"Get down!" he yelled at Jojo. He looked in the rearview mirror. Where was Davis? Tom and Denis? The Mercedes roared up behind them.

"Are you all right?" Jack said.

"I'm fine!" Jojo yelped, slouched low in the seat. "What's going on? Did they just *shoot* at us? Who is it?"

Jack gritted his teeth. The Mustang looked like it could haul ass but it was nothing compared to the Mercedes, which slammed into the back of them, sending the Mustang momentarily out of control before Jack managed to get the car straightened again.

He took another turn which led them through an industrial complex, lots of abandoned looking buildings and storage facilities. He needed to get them back to a main street. There was no way he was going to be able to outpace the Benz, but perhaps he could outmaneuver it. He turned left, hoping he would come full circle back to the main road they had been on, but was instead greeted with the sight of a dead-end, abandoned-looking warehouses on both sides, all sorts of debris and trash littering the road.

Shit, he thought, though he kept it to himself. He didn't want to scare Jojo any more than she already was—he would do whatever he could to get them out of this situation safely. Yet he was now faced with the very real possibility that that might not happen. They were trapped. The Mercedes had also made the turn and was now accelerating toward them.

"Jack?" Jojo said, her voice quavering. "What's happening?"

He looked in the rearview mirror at the fast-approaching car. "Just sit tight." He put the Mustang in reverse, then stepped on the gas.

The two cars slammed into each other, Jack and Jojo lurching against their seatbelts at the moment of impact. The heavier Mercedes absorbed the force and pushed the Mustang forward, even though Jack kept his foot down on the accelerator.

Suddenly—the Mercedes stopped. Jack hit the brakes and put the car in park. He looked in the sideview mirror and saw the driver's side door open. A man got out. Jack squinted. Where had he seen him . . .

Yesterday. At the delicatessen. As the man moved closer, gun at his side, there was no doubt in Jack's mind that this had been one of the men at the booth next to them. He'd taken notice of them, but only because he thought they were being rude, checking out Jojo. The thought that these people might be following them had never occurred to him, and he was furious at himself, but he needed to keep his focus if he was going to get them out of this situation. Tom and Denis were nowhere in sight.

The man was right there, gun pointed at the window. He fired once. Jojo shrieked and Jack flinched but the bulletproof glass held. The man fired again, and this time, the bullet splintered the glass. One more shot was all it would take.

Jack lowered the window about four inches and put the car in drive, but didn't step on the gas. "What . . . what are you doing?" Jojo whispered. As the car rolled forward, the man jammed the gun in through the space in the window, a grin on his face as if he had already won.

Wrong, Jack thought as he grabbed the muzzle of the handgun and twisted it away from his body, wrenching the man's arms so the barrel was now facing the steering wheel.

He stomped on the accelerator and the car shot forward. The man had the choice to either hang on and get his arms ripped off or let go—the gun fell in Jack's lap, and he looked back and saw the man sprawled on the ground, the two other guys he was with were jumping out of the Mercedes, guns drawn.

Jack threw the car in reverse and gunned it. There was a sickening thud as the car steamrolled the first guy. The other two scrambled to take cover behind the Mercedes' open doors, but Jack let the back of the Mustang slam into the black car again.

"Get down," he said to Jojo as he put his window all the way down. "All the way in the floor well. Stay as low as possible."

He watched out the sideview mirror to time it just right—when the second man stepped around the open driver's side door toward the Mustang, Jack leaned out the window and quickly fired off three shots. It had been a long time since he'd last shot a gun. But the man fell and made no move to get up.

Where was the third guy?

Everything seemed strangely quiet. Jack stared intently at the sideview mirror, but there was no movement. He opened the car door and got out.

"Jack," Jojo said. "Don't . . ."

He put his finger to his lips, his eyes locked on the Mercedes. There was a flash of movement from behind the open passenger side door, and Jack dropped down to the ground, using the Mustang as cover, but not before he heard the sound of a shot and felt a searing pain on his right arm.

Shit, he thought, gritting his teeth. He looked at his arm, the fabric on the outer sleeve of shirt torn. The bullet had glanced him, it hadn't gone in. He tried to channel the pain into focus. There was a crushed Miller High Life can on the ground a few feet from him, so he snatched it and threw it toward the passenger side of the Mercedes. He jumped up, the can still arcing through the air, the third man losing his focus for a moment, his gaze skyward. Jack fired off four shots and the man crumpled to the ground.

He dropped the gun and ran over to the Mustang's passenger side door. "Jojo! Are you all right?" He leaned in and helped her get up from the car's floor well. Once out of the car, he brushed her hair back and kissed her forehead.

"Jack, you're bleeding," she said. "Did you get shot?"

"The bullet just grazed me. It's nothing."

He wrapped his arms around her, the pain in his own arm flaring. He welcomed the pain though, which cut like a laser through his brain fog. That had been too close. Way too close. After a moment, they both stood up and surveyed the damage.

Two destroyed cars. Well, the Mercedes appeared to have made out better than the Mustang, but it was also riddled with bullet holes. Three bodies.

"These guys were in the restaurant yesterday," Jack said. "At the deli. Sitting right next to us, and I didn't give it a second thought." He clenched his jaw, unable to believe how stupid he had been. To just write it off as some guys checking out his girlfriend—what a careless error.

Jojo's eyes widened. "Oh my god," she said. "You're right—I didn't even realize it. How did they . . ." Her voice trailed off. "I thought we would be safer here."

"I need to take pictures," Jack said. He felt completely detached as he took photographs of the three bodies, as well as the scene around them. He was aware of what he was doing, and of the danger that his life and Jojo's had just been in, yet it was almost as if he were disassociating as he took the photos, looked down at the blank faces of the men who only moments ago had tried to murder him.

He had just finished when two black SUVs screeched to a halt at the end of the road and then turned onto the dead-end street, coming to a stop right behind the Mercedes.

Davis jumped out and rushed over to Jojo and Jack. "What the hell happened?" he said.

"I could ask you the same thing," Jack said through gritted teeth. He reached for Jojo's hand. "I'm putting her in the SUV." He didn't wait for Davis to respond; he led her over to the vehicle and helped her into the back. She was trembling a little and Jack could see fear in her eyes. "Hey," he said, waiting for her to meet his gaze before he continued. "You're safe here."

"Where are you going?"

"I'll be right back; I just need to go talk to Davis."

She nodded, her eyes still wide. Jack gave her hand a squeeze. "I'll be right back, I promise."

Several other agents had arrived, people Jack didn't recognize. They swarmed the scene, guns drawn.

"Are you all right?" Davis asked. "You have some injuries." He nodded to Jack's right arm. "Looks like you were grazed by a bullet."

"Yeah, I'll be okay."

"This is serious shit, Jack," Davis said, shaking his head. "As I'm sure you're well aware. Run me through everything once—I'll record it and you won't have to talk about it again."

Jack told him what happened, leaving nothing out. When he was finished, Davis took several photos of Jack's injuries.

Sirens in the distance. Four local police cars pulled up. Jack looked at the Mercedes, with its shattered window, the windshield pocked with a few bullet holes, but it had held. The Mustang fared far worse, the back end smashed, the rear window nearly gone, bullet holes on both the driver and the passenger side. Things could've ended much differently.

One of the police officers made his way over and introduced himself as the chief of police. "What happened here?"

"Three Chinese nationals tried to kill me and Jojo, who is the daughter of Wang Yang, the president of China."

The officer's eyes widened as he looked at Jack, and then around, presumably, for Jojo.

"She's in the SUV," Jack said. "She's shaken up, but okay."

"This is a matter for the FBI to handle," Davis said. "Jack just gave me his version of what happened, and I'll send you over the recording. If you have any questions, let us know."

The police chief nodded and wiped at his brow, clearly relieved that he wouldn't have to deal with this mess.

* * *

Three hours later, after seven stitches, a butterfly bandage on his forehead, and a mediocre hamburger from the hospital's cafeteria, Jack and Jojo found themselves in the back of Davis's SUV, heading to Sedona.

By now, Jack knew the rest of the story, or as much as he would ever probably find out: Paul's phone had been tapped, and a signal jammer had been used so neither Davis or Tom and Denis were able to track Jack after they'd exited off the highway into Needles.

Jack's right arm throbbed lightly. He'd been offered opiate pain-killers at the hospital, but declined, instead opting for the extra strength ibuprofen. He'd be sore tomorrow, though.

The black phone beeped in his pocket, and Jack shifted slightly to retrieve it, the message a five-word apology from Cooper: *Sorry Jack. I'm so sorry.*

He stared at the words. Of course they were sorry. But they were also relieved, because neither he nor Jojo had been injured or killed. The threat of Zhang Zhong and the group he was leading had not been taken seriously enough, but Jack would do whatever was in his power to ensure that nothing like this would happen again. He wrote a message back to Cooper:

> *Please forward all these pictures to President Wang Yang and President Sutton. Please also attach the following message: "I want your signatures re Trade Framework within the hour. Otherwise, I'll release to the media pictures with the following caption: President Wang and President Sutton have still not signed the trade frame-work agreement Jack Gold has submitted to them. Today, an attempt was made on Jack's life and the daughter of President Wang. The attempt was made in America by Chinese nationals."*

He hoped that was clear enough.

CHAPTER 9

Paul lived on Red Rock Loop Rd, in a two-level, Tuscan-inspired home, tucked in front of a towering cliff of red rock, as picturesque as anything you'd see on a postcard. As Davis parked behind Paul's 911 Porsche, Jack suddenly remembered their luggage.

"Shit," he said. "Our luggage is still in the Mustang."

"It'll be here in an hour," Davis replied. "They had to pry open the trunk."

Paul came out of the house as Jack and Jojo got out of the SUV. "Hey!" he called, waving. "Wasn't sure what time you guys were going to show up and I tried to get in touch, Jack, but my messages weren't getting through for some reason." He eyed Davis, the other SUVs in his driveway. "Uh . . . I thought you were renting a car and driving yourself." Paul looked at him more closely. "And . . . what happened to your *face?*"

"Yeah, I'll explain all that later," Jack said, giving his brother a hug. "Good to see you. I'd like you to meet Jojo."

Paul grinned as he shook Jojo's hand. "It's a pleasure," he said. "An honor! So nice to meet you, Jojo. Welcome to America; I hope you've been having a great time so far."

Jojo laughed. "That's one way of putting it."

"This is Davis," Jack said. "Davis, my brother, Paul."

"You the chaperone?" Paul asked.

Davis did not return his smile. "I work with the FBI," he said. "And Jack and Jojo did rent a car and were going to drive themselves, but there was a bit of trouble along the way. You're the owner of this property?"

Paul's eyebrows shot up and he looked at Jack, then back to Davis. "Yes, sir," he said. "The one and only."

"Then I'd like your permission to station a few people around the grounds for security purposes."

Paul frowned. "Well, I'm more than happy to give you *my* permission, but . . . good luck with the neighbors."

Davis looked around. Aside from the two drones above them and the helicopter further in the distance, there was no one else around.

"You'll have to excuse my brother," Jack said. "He's always had a quirky sense of humor."

Paul looked up, too. "Is that helicopter here for you guys?"

"Yes."

"Jesus." He let out a low whistle. "Then it's *definitely* beer and tequila time. I'm making lamb tacos. Hope everyone's hungry!"

Jack and Jojo followed him inside. The house itself was stunning, with its high ceilings, exposed beams, windows in a range of sizes meant to show off the impressive views from anywhere you stood in the house. Everything had a warm earth tone, from the brown leather sectional in the living room to honey-colored hardwood floors. Even the kitchen fit the motif, with a deep bronze faucet and tan brown granite countertops.

"This is quite the place," Jack said. "Paul, you haven't done so bad for yourself."

Paul turned from the fridge, three beers in hand. "Let's take these and go sit on the deck," he said. "You have some explaining to do."

They went out on the deck, with its stunning view of the red rock, dotted here and there with juniper trees and pinyon pine. They sat on thick cushions atop wrought iron chairs. Paul opened a beer and handed it to Jojo, then did the same for Jack. He opened his own, took a long swig, and then said, "So. Why all the FBI? I assume it has to do with what you did over there in China, Jack. Getting your face plastered all over TV."

"That's part of it," Jack said. "Jojo is the daughter of the president of China. And three guys tried to kill us earlier today."

"Seriously?"

"Seriously. Three Chinese nationals in a blacked-out Mercedes. Chased us down, tried to shoot us."

"What the fuck, Jack, that's like out of *Fast and Furious* or something. You're lucky you had security with you!"

"No," Jojo said, before Jack could respond. "We didn't have anyone there; it was just the two of us. And Jack managed to somehow get one of the guns away from the guys."

Paul's mouth fell open. "Wait—you *killed* someone?"

"There was no other choice. I had to. If I didn't, they would've killed us." It felt strange to say that, though he would do it again without second thought were he to find himself in the same situation.

Paul leaned back in his chair and regarded both of them, an expression of awe on his face that Jack was not accustomed to seeing. "You are unbelievable." He grinned. "I better go get the tequila."

Jack and Jojo laughed. "I like him," Jojo whispered once Paul was out of earshot. "Not nearly as much as you!" she added, when Jack raised an eyebrow.

Paul returned with a bottle of tequila and three shot glasses, a perplexed expression on his face.

"What's up?" Jack asked.

"Uh . . . it would appear there are two guys in all black, armed with M16s, in my front yard?"

"About time," Jack said. "I guess it took us nearly getting killed for them to take the threat seriously." He nodded to the tequila. "I'll take a shot of that."

"What do you mean?"

"I mean that I've had a shitty day and I'd like to at least get a little buzzed."

Paul poured him a shot. "No, what do you mean about them not taking the threat seriously?" He handed the shot glass to Jack, who tossed it back, barely tasting it, just feeling the residual burn in his esophagus.

"I meant before the whole thing happened today. It shouldn't have gotten that far—those guys should have been stopped long before they were ever able to follow us to L.A.. I told the president this. I'm glad that they realize the gravity here, but I'm not happy that it took us almost getting killed."

Jack took a deep breath. He didn't want to keep going on about it, he didn't want Jojo to have to keep reliving the whole horrible situation. The more he thought about it, though, the more he realized how it was such a profound failure on many people's parts—including himself. He should have at least mentioned the men at the deli to Davis, he should not have just dismissed it. That was certainly not a mistake that he would be making again.

Paul poured another shot for Jack, and then one for himself and Jojo, which they all did at the same time, followed by a big swig of beer.

Jack felt the edges of his vision soften, the stress of the day beginning to dilute. He felt safe here at his brother's house, with the security presence outside. He could let his guard down here, a welcome respite from the last six hours.

"How's work going?" Jack asked.

Paul nodded enthusiastically. "It's great. Couldn't be better, actually. You want to check out my studio?"

"I would love that," Jojo said. "I'd also love to hear about your work."

They followed Paul off the deck, around the back of the house to his attached workshop. "I'm an industrial designer and I make furniture, mostly, and some art. Jack said you're a sculptor?"

"I am."

"I'd love to check out your work some time."

Like the rest of the house, Paul's studio had high ceilings and lots of windows. There were chairs and bookshelves in various stages of completion, as well as some less conventional pieces.

"Tell me about this pyramid," Jojo said, walking over to a large stainless-steel structure in the corner of the room.

"Obviously, still a work in progress," Paul said, "but someone wanted one to place in front of their home."

"Interesting. I like it. Stainless steel?"

"Yes, primarily. I do the majority of this sort of work with stainless steel, but I also use ancillary materials like bamboo, glass, and leather."

Jojo nodded. "I could use some shelves for my statues. That would free up some space."

"Shelves are my specialty!" Paul exclaimed. "Just tell me the sort of thing you're thinking of and I can make some sketches and suggest materials."

"I know a ton of people in China who would like your work," Jojo said. "You should have a show in Shanghai! That would be great."

Jack wandered around the studio while Jojo and Paul talked about art shows. Though he was no expert in these matters, Jack had to admit that Paul was very talented at what he did.

As they walked back to the deck, Jack's black phone beeped. It was a message from Cooper, informing him that both presidents had signed the documents.

"Yes," Jack said out loud as he typed a quick reply.

"What is it?" Jojo asked.

"I sent your dad and Sutton an ultimatum regarding the trade negotiations framework. I sent them pictures of what happened earlier and the story I was going to send to press unless they signed the framework within the hour. They signed."

Paul let out a low whistle. "Look at you, playing hardball with two world leaders. Damn, Jack. You're not messing around. This calls for another shot! Oh yeah, and then dinner."

For dinner, they had lamb tacos, along with another shot of tequila, at least for Jack and Paul; Jojo had another beer. There was a knock at the door right as they were finishing, but it only turned out to be Davis, dropping off their luggage.

"You want to come in for a beer, man?" Paul asked. "Shot of tequila? Both? Hell, after the day you guys have had, I think both could probably do you some good!"

"Thanks, but no," Davis said. "You all have a good night."

Though Jack could tell that Paul was eager to stay up and drink, reminisce about the old days and speculate about what the future held, Jack needed to call it an early night. His arm was starting to throb and his whole body felt sore. Paul showed them their upstairs room and then said goodnight, giving first Jack, then Jojo, a hug.

"I think I'm going to take a shower," Jojo said. "I feel like I need to wash this day off of me."

She opened her suitcase and took out a few things before making her way into the bathroom across the hall.

Jack sat down on the queen size bed. He couldn't wait until he was lying underneath the covers, head sinking into one of those pillows, arms around Jojo, blessed sleep descending. He went over to his suitcase, lifting it up onto the bench at the foot of the bed. He planned to get something to change into after his shower, and his toothbrush, but he paused before he had the case open. There was, in the righthand corner, a hole. Jack frowned, running is finger over the tiny crater. A bullet hole.

Jesus Christ, he thought, as he opened the suitcase to see if anything inside had been damaged.

CHAPTER 10

Jack awoke the next day to the sound of his black phone beeping. He picked it up, looking at the time. Seven in the morning. The message was from Cooper, short and to the point:

> *President Wang would like you and Jojo to return to Beijing today, by 12 noon latest.*
>
> *You'll fly from Flagstaff Airport*

He put the phone back on the bedside table as Jojo began to stir beside him. "Was that your phone?" she asked with a yawn. "Or was that beeping sound part of the dream I was having?"

"It was my phone," Jack said. "Your dad wants us to return to Beijing today by noon. Understandably. So, we don't really have much choice."

Jojo sat up, stretching. "You know, it's funny, I was a little afraid to come to America because of the guns here. And yet, it ends up being the Chinese using them." She shook her head. "How's your arm?"

"Sore," Jack said. "But nothing too bad. I guess we better get up; we don't have much time left."

They made their way out to the kitchen, following the enticing aroma of strong coffee. The coffee pot was full, and Jack found two mugs in the cupboard.

"Where's your brother?" Jojo asked as she poured cream into her coffee.

"I'm not sure." Jack took a sip of his coffee, his gaze going to the window above the sink. "Oh, he's out on the deck."

He and Jojo took their cups and joined Paul in the cool, early morning weather.

"Good morning," Paul said. "You found the coffee, I see. Sleep well?"

"That bed is so comfortable," Jojo said. "This whole place is incredible, it's like some sort of retreat. I love it here."

"Well, Jojo, you are welcome here any time. I'm so glad that you and Jack get to stay for a little while, there's a ton of stuff I can't wait to show you guys—"

"Uh . . ." Jack interrupted, throwing a look Jojo's way. Paul frowned. "What's up?"

"Well, I received a text message this morning informing me that Jojo's dad wants us to leave by noon today."

"Whoa," Paul said. "I guess when the president speaks, you listen." But Jack could tell his brother was disappointed. Paul sighed. "Not the news I was expecting to hear. So . . . go put your shoes on. We're going for a little hike. It's not even seven-thirty yet; we have plenty of time. I won't get us lost, I promise, and I'll bring coffee."

They went inside and quickly changed and put their shoes on. They followed Paul through his backyard and then took a left onto a well-traveled singletrack trail, that wound its way through acacia and live oak. They began to ascend the mountain. Paul led the way, with Jojo behind him, moving with ease on the steep trail. Jack's arm began to throb; he hadn't taken any ibuprofen yet and also still felt half-asleep—hiking a mountain hadn't been on his agenda, at least not right off the bat.

But there really wasn't another time for them to do this, if they had to be out of here by noon, and he knew this was an experience Jojo would enjoy. If he could survive yesterday, then this should be a walk in the park. *Or a walk up a mountainside,* Jack thought, smiling.

"I won't make you go all the way to the top," Paul said, "though that was my plan when I thought we had more time. But this is a good lookout right here—whoa!" He jumped as they turned the corner. "Uh . . ." He looked over his shoulder at Jack, who was still a few steps behind.

There was a security agent, dressed in all black, holding an M16. Fifteen feet in front of him was another similarly dressed man, lying on the cliff's edge on his stomach, looking through the scope of a sniper rifle.

"So, I would surmise that you guys are still in danger," Paul said.

Jack nodded. "It would appear that way."

Jojo ignored the two men and took in the full view. The sky was an endless deep blue, with cotton ball clouds to the east. Below them, the land stretched as far as they could see, dwellings dotted here and there, cactus, shrubs, and more redrock mountains in the distance.

"This is stunning," Jojo said. She took a deep breath. "And the air is so clean. It must be inspiring to live here."

"Yeah, it is," Paul said.

"Do you hike up here often with your coffee?"

"It's my second favorite thing to do. My first is to come up here at sunset with a beer, which is what I hoped we'd be able to do this evening. But let's at least have a cup of coffee."

He took his backpack off and pulled out a thermos and three enamel camping mugs. Once everyone had their beverage, Paul held his cup up.

"Cheers," he said.

"Cheers." They toasted each other and enjoyed the coffee and the view. Jack tried to pretend the two FBI agents weren't right there.

The descent was easy and quick, and by the time they arrived back to Paul's, Jack could feel his stomach rumbling.

"Plenty of time left for breakfast," Paul said. He took out a pan out from a cupboard and set it on the stove. "Jack, you're going to love what I have in store for you. Jojo, you too."

"And what might that be?" Jack asked as he poured himself another coffee.

"I went to Whole Foods a few months ago and there was a guy outside with samples of his own pasture-raised heritage pork bacon. So, being the selective Jew that I am, I tried it. And it was very tasty! I had to have more. He's now my bacon guy."

Jack and Jojo laughed. "Your own bacon guy," Jack said. "Damn. I wish we had one. The bacon in Shanghai sucks."

They sat at the counter, drinking coffee, watching Paul as he threw together quite the spread. He sliced up some cantaloupe and some strawberries, which he put in a glass bowl, and then added some blueberries. He slid the bowl across the counter.

"Snack on this," he said. "I'll get the main course started."

Jack watched as his brother cut up shiitake mushrooms and green onions and then set them to sauté in a cast iron skillet with some olive oil. He cracked six eggs into a separate bowl and scrambled them.

"That pan is ready for those eggs," Jack said. Paul nodded and poured the eggs over the mushrooms and onions. "And some salt and pepper," Jack added.

Jojo glanced at him. "Are you being the bossy older brother? He seems to be doing just fine on his own."

Jack and Paul exchanged a look, smiling. "I know how it must appear," Jack said. "But, it's not *really* me being a bossy older brother."

"Jack has always had the uncanny ability to know the right thing to do about pretty much anything. Cooking included. Which, up until recently, has not been my forte." Paul dropped two slices of toast into the toaster. "Just ask our dad. Have you met him yet?"

Jojo shook her head. "No, but I'd like to."

"Our dad will tell you how Jack has always been able to see several moves ahead, like life was just one big chess game and he was the Grand Master. So, I learned pretty early on to listen to Jack."

"I see," Jojo said. "And I agree—Jack is very perceptive."

"Have you talked to Dad?" Paul asked. "Does he know you're here?"

"No, I didn't tell him we were making the trip. Which is a good thing, I guess, since we're leaving. Better give those eggs a stir."

"I mean," Paul said, as he stirred the eggs, "you have to witness it first-hand, Jojo. I'm willing to bet, had it been me or anyone else in the car when those guys started shooting, we'd be dead." He looked at Jack. "Can you tell me the details? How it all went down? Or is it like classified information or something?"

"I can tell you. But you should feed me first."

Paul cut the omelet in the pan and dished up three plates, along with the thick slices of bacon and salsa. He buttered the two slices of toast and gave one to Jojo and one to Jack, before putting another slice in the toaster for himself.

"This does look good," Jack said. He took a few bites. "Okay. I can give you the rundown."

Paul sat and listened intently as Jack replayed the scene, the best to his memory. When he got to the part about tossing the crushed can, Paul raised his fork and shook it, a triumphant smile on his face.

"See?" he said to Jojo. "Who would've thought of that? You weren't planning that, right?"

"No. But I knew I needed something to distract him if I was going to have a chance to get a clean shot." He put his fork down and rubbed Jojo's back. "But honestly, the most important thing to me was that we get out of there safely. It's my job to protect you."

Jojo smiled and leaned over and gave him a kiss on the cheek. "You did a great job. You do a great job with everything."

When they were finished eating, Jack and Jojo went and got their things together. Paul asked if he could ride to the airport with them, which, after getting the okay from Davis, Jack said was fine.

"How are you going to get back?" Jack asked.

"I'll just take an Uber. Which airport are you going to?"

"Flagstaff."

Paul frowned. "I don't think commercial flights go out of Flagstaff."

"They don't," Davis said, "but Flagstaff's runway is about nine thousand feet long; their plane only needs about six thousand three hundred."

"Wait, wait," Paul said. "*Their* plane?" He looked at Jack. "You have your own plane?"

"No, it's not ours. We're not jet-setting all over the globe. But when we travel, yes, we use it."

"I want to see this plane of yours."

They arrived at the airport about forty-five minutes later, and Paul immediately hopped out of the back of the SUV and made a beeline for the plane.

"You coming with us?" Jack asked.

"I wish. I was just hoping I could check it out. You're traveling in some serious style, Jack. Damn. I don't even know what to say."

"Unfortunately," Jack said, "I think right now we have to say goodbye. I'm really sorry we had to cut the visit short." He gave his brother a hug. "Next time we'll have a longer visit, I promise. Whether it's here or you come see us in China."

"Yes!" Jojo chimed in as Paul gave her a hug. "You should definitely come visit us in China."

"Oh, I will. Do I get to fly a plane like this over?"

"Of course," Jojo said. "Thank you for having us, Paul. I'm so glad I got to meet part of Jack's family."

Jack waved to his brother one last time, and then Paul trotted down the stairs, which were then moved back and the plane's door shut.

It was time to go back to China.

CHAPTER 11

It was a beautiful day when they arrived back in Beijing—so much so that, as they drove to their hotel, they could see people outside, taking pictures of the fluffy clouds, the blue sky—a rare view. Usually, the pollution made such a view impossible.

The boutique hotel had been transformed in their absence, the front of it cordoned off with a massive fifteen-foot-tall fence, covered with bamboo. Davis stopped the SUV at the gate and put the window down, pressed a button on the call box, and the gate slid open.

Davis drove through onto a newly laid cobblestone driveway. To his right, Jack saw a large area that had been cleared and filled with soil, just waiting for something to be planted. A gravel path led from the garden to the hotel, and a wrought iron table and chairs had been placed underneath the shade of a willow tree.

Inside, though, they were in for even more of a surprise. The hotel had been completely transformed.

"Wow," Jojo said. Most of the interior walls had been removed, leaving an enormous, wide open space. There was a living area, decorated with two large Persian rugs and a sectional sofa and two leather recliners. Further back were Jojo's two room dividers, gold leaf screens with bamboo flowers, arranged in front of the back windows, which helped give the massive room less of an industrial feel.

"That's smart," Jack said. "Putting those screens there. It's good feng shui—they'll stop the energy from coming in the front door and leaving via the window."

Jojo looked at him and started to laugh. "Oh my god," she said. "You're more Chinese than I am."

They continued to explore their new home. At the far end, near the bamboo screens, Jojo's statues had been meticulously laid out on their pedestals and looked as if they were ready for an art show. The kitchen had been completely renovated—there was a new Sub-Zero refrigerator, bamboo floors, and polished granite counters.

"They really did a great job," Jack said. "I'm no professional when it comes to this sort of thing, but I'm impressed."

There was a knock at the door, which seemed to echo throughout the space. Jack and Jojo looked at each other.

"Are you expecting someone?" Jack asked.

She shook her head. They both walked over and Jack opened the door.

It was Wang Yang. He had Mini with him.

"Dad!" Jojo exclaimed, and she threw her arms around him.

"I'm so glad you're back, and everyone's safe," he said as he wrapped his arms around her. Jack looked away and patted the dog; though it was maybe the first time Wang had hugged his daughter, Jack almost felt like he was intruding on the moment.

"It was so horrible. I wouldn't even be alive right now if it weren't for Jack."

Wang let go of Jojo and held out a hand to Jack. Jack shook it, but then felt himself being pulled in for a hug, too.

"Thank you," Wang whispered. "I saw all the pictures and heard a live audio of what transpired. You saved my daughter's life. You have my eternal gratitude."

They went over and sat down in the living area. Mini jumped up and curled himself on Jojo's lap. "I understand you were shot in the arm, Jack."

"I was. Just grazed, though, nothing serious. A few stitches."

Wang looked at him curiously. "May I see?"

"Sure." Jack took off his shirt and removed the bandage. "I should probably keep the bandage off now anyway, let it get some air."

Wang looked at the stitches closely, then nodded. "It looks like it's healing nicely. That is good. I'll send someone by in a few days to take them out."

"Thank you."

"So," Wang continued, "I'm not sure how much you've been paying attention to the news, but the police department had to release a report and photos about the incident to the press. We decided to issue a statement as well. We used one of the photos Davis took of your injuries. It's quite the striking image; it's gotten a significant number of views online, I've been informed."

Jack slipped his shirt back over his head. "I'm not sure whether that's good or bad."

"I think it's a good thing," Wang said. "The people of China are really rooting for you."

"Well, except those that are trying to murder me."

"Yes, well, we are doing all that we can to determine who the three men were and if they had any connection to Zhang Zhong. But more importantly, I want you and Jojo to know that you are safe here. Every precaution has been taken." Wang stood up from the couch. "I know you two just got in, so I'm not going to stay. Explore your new place, and let me know if there's anything else that you need. Jack, take a day or two to rest and then let's plan on getting together to talk about a few security matters."

"Absolutely," Jack said. "Thank you again for everything."

After Wang Yang left, Jack and Jojo decided to christen their new bathroom by taking a bath together. Upstairs, they discovered that not only had the bathroom been fully renovated to include double sinks and a deep soaking tub, but they also had an office suite, complete with matching desks and filing cabinets.

So far as homes went, Jack thought, this one wasn't so bad at all.

*   *   *

He awoke the next morning to the sound of knocking at the door. Jack looked at his phone as he stood up and saw that it was almost nine o'clock. He pulled on a pair of jeans and a t-shirt as he quietly made his way out of the room and down to the front door.

"We received this at the embassy a little while ago," Davis said, handing him a thick manila envelope. On the front someone had written in red: *Eyes Only, Jack Gold.* There was also the stamp of the U.S. State Department. "Figured you'd want it sooner rather than later."

"Thanks," Jack said, though he had no idea exactly what the envelope might contain.

He said goodbye to Davis and went and sat on the sofa, positioned so he could see Jojo if she came downstairs. The envelope contained a handwritten note, on thick, cream-colored stationary: *An early wedding present. Love, Cam and Bob Sutton. PS: Contact Gerard at Harry Winston in Beijing.*

Jack frowned and stuck his hand back into the envelope. At the bottom was a small velvet drawstring pouch. He pulled it out and opened it.

Inside was a deep red pear-shaped diamond.

It was stunning.

But he only had a moment to admire it, because he heard Jojo's footsteps on the stairs. He slipped the diamond back into the pouch and put it, along with the note, into his pocket. He folded up the envelope.

"Good morning," he said.

"I can't believe I slept so late." Jojo looked at the envelope. "What's that?"

"Davis just stopped by; this came for me via the State Department. Just trade negotiation stuff." Jack gave her a kiss. "It's only nine o'clock, and considering the past few days we've had, you deserve some rest."

"I know, I just really need to get back into the swing of things. I've been feeling a little unsettled, so I'd really like to focus on my work today. If that's okay with you?"

"Of course it is. Do whatever you need to do. I'll go see your dad about the security stuff today." He went back upstairs and retrieved his black phone and let Cooper know he wanted to meet with President Wang and also make a visit to Harry Winston.

He and Jojo made breakfast together, having discovered yesterday that the fridge and the pantry was fully stocked with all the things they liked. After eating, Jack went and took a shower, shaved, and dressed in a dark blue suit and red tie. He retrieved the note from the Suttons and the velvet pouch with the diamond, which he had hid in the small drawer of his bedside table. Last thing he needed was his pair of Creative Officine shoes, which he carried downstairs and left by the door. Jojo whistled when she saw him.

"You look good in a suit."

She came over and ran her fingers down the lapels of his suit. Jack smiled down at her. "I'm off, babe. I hope you have a great day. Call me if you need anything."

They gave each other a long, lingering kiss, the sort of which Jack would've liked to follow up with heading right back up to bed, but he had places to be, and he knew Jojo was eager to get back to her work.

Davis was waiting for him when he stepped outside. "Good morning, Jack. How are you?"

"Hi Davis. I never thought I'd say this, but I somehow feel safer in China than in America."

They drove twenty minutes to one of the most elegant hotels in China, the Peninsula Beijing. Within the hotel was the Peninsula Arcade, where dozens of high-end shops, including Harry Winston, were located. Davis walked with Jack up to the entrance, but remained at the door, a few feet from a Chinese guard who was stationed there.

"Good luck," Davis said with a little smile.

Jack stepped into the luxury shop, home to some of the most exquisite jewelry in the world. A tall, attractive woman approached him, asking how she could help.

"I was hoping to speak with Gerard," Jack said. "I was referred by one of his clients."

A look of recognition crossed the woman's face. "Of course, Mr. Gold," she said. "Please just wait a moment."

Jack walked over to one of the display cases which held a variety of diamond rings on platinum bands, nestled in white velvet ring trays. While they were all inarguably beautiful, he knew he had made the right choice in going with the red diamond.

"Mr. Gold?"

Jack turned. A man in an impeccable gray suit and navy blue tie held his hand out. "Gerard," he said. "It's a pleasure to meet you. Bob said you'd be dropping by; this is an honor."

Jack returned the handshake. "The honor's mine, really," he said. "I never thought I'd have enough money to even enter your esteemed establishment."

Gerard smiled. "Well. Here you are. How may I help you?"

"I believe I'm in need of an engagement ring."

"Excellent. I see you've found some of what we have to offer. Did anything in this case strike your fancy?"

"Actually," Jack said, reaching into his inner jacket pocket, "I have a stone and was hoping you could assist me with the setting."

"Absolutely. May I see the stone?"

Jack handed him the diamond. Gerard pulled a loupe from his pocket and put it to his right eye. He held his hand up, the diamond resting on his palm. For a moment, he said nothing. "Where did you get this?" he finally asked.

"Uh . . . Bob helped me," Jack said.

Gerard nodded. "It's fancy vivid and would score a number one on the Argyle scoring system."

"That all sounds like gibberish to me."

"That's the best. Three and a half carats." He walked over behind the counter and to a digital scale. He delicately placed the diamond on it. The display read 3.55. "Mr. Gold," Gerard said. "This is a *very* nice diamond." His eyes sparkled. "Would you like to know how much it is worth?"

He started to say yes, but stopped. He had a feeling it wouldn't matter to Jojo, and also, that if he knew the exact amount, he probably wouldn't even feel comfortable walking around with it in his pocket. "No. It doesn't matter. What matters to me is finding the perfect setting to best showcase the diamond's beauty."

"A diamond like this, it won't be hard. Did you have a particular setting in mind?"

"Well, the person who will wear this is a sculptor. So I was thinking maybe black-matted Tungsten with six-claw prongs. But, I'm open to suggestions, too. I know graphene or carbon fiber or titanium might be good choices, too."

"Let's have a seat over here," Gerard said, gesturing to a small desk in front of an inset wall display of necklaces and time pieces. Jack sat in one of the high-backed leather chairs, across from Gerard, who took a pad of paper from the desk and a pen from his inside jacket pocket.

"I think your gut is right, Mr. Gold. Tungsten would be the best. It's the strongest and the color in matte black is very nice, particularly with a diamond such as yours." Jack watched as he sketched out the ring and setting. "It would look like this—a slightly bigger band than normal. The prongs would be clearly visible holding the diamond in place, which I think is a nice touch. It will be strong and its weight is comparable to platinum." Gerard regarded the sketch. "The look would be somewhat industrial. Is that okay with you?"

He turned the pad so it was facing Jack. "It's perfect," he said. "You nailed it. Thank you."

"No," Gerard said with a smile. "*You* knew everything you wanted—I just sketched it out. So, the Tungsten is from China, but the setting will be made in Los Angeles."

Jack laughed. "Are you kidding me?"

"No," Gerard said, frowning. "Is that . . . is that a problem?"

"No. I'm just originally from LA, so it's funny that . . . well, never mind. Is there anything else you need from me?"

"I think I have everything—actually, no, I do need one more thing. Do you happen to know the ring size?"

"Yes. Fifteen point two millimeters. So a four-and-a-half U.S. size, I believe."

Gerard nodded, a skeptical look on his face. "I have to tell you, Mr. Gold—Tungsten rings cannot be resized. One of the few drawbacks when working with this material. Where did you get the measurement done, if you don't mind me asking?"

"Cartier. In Beverly Hills."

The answer seemed to satisfy Gerard. He wrote out a receipt and then exchanged WeChat with Jack so he could notify him when the ring was ready.

"It should be about six days," he said. "Though it could be sooner; we will be in touch when it's ready."

"That's perfect." Jack slipped the receipt into his pocket and shook hands with Gerard.

Now it was time to go meet with Wang Yang.

*　*　*

One of the first people Jack met when he arrived at Zhongnanhai was an armed military officer named Liang, who was head of the area's security regiment. He led Jack down a hallway to an unseen elevator. "I'd like to express, on behalf of the regiment, our gratitude about what you did to save the life of the president's daughter. We all saw the photos and heard a translation of the live feed, as well as your debriefing." The elevator doors closed and Liang pressed the only button on the wall panel, which said "down" in Chinese. Jack's stomach did a little flip as the elevator began its descent.

"We'd all love to see how you did it. A reenactment? I think it would be educational for the men in the regiment."

"I think I could do that," Jack said, a bit surprised at the request. But Liang really did seem to be looking at him in admiration, and Jack couldn't help but feel flattered. "We'd have to do it without Jojo, of course. I don't want to put her through that."

Liang nodded. "Yes, yes, absolutely."

The elevator stopped and the doors opened. In front of Jack was a large steel door that led to a massive operations room. From where he stood, he could see a large conference room and rows of cubicles. Beyond that appeared to be several smaller conference rooms and at least half a dozen large television monitors. The walls were painted white, which gave everything a very stark, modern feel, in sharp contrast to the traditional Chinese architecture above them. Jack recognized the room for what it was—a bunker that could protect its occupants from a nuclear strike.

Wang Yang had been talking with three men in uniform, but he stopped his conversation and walked over to Jack. "Thanks for coming down," he said. "You're the first foreigner to visit the area."

"It's an honor."

"I have a few people I'd like to introduce you to." He led Jack over to the men he had just been speaking to. "Jack Gold, this is General Ma, General Li, and General Lin."

"Nice to meet you," Jack said as he shook each of their hands. General Ma and General Li were both older, probably in their sixties, Jack guessed. General Lin appeared to be in his early fifties, perhaps.

They went into the large conference room. "The three people you neutralized had known relations with Zhang Zhong," General Lin began. "We traced back all their phones calls and WeChat messages. A search of their homes found no communications with Zhang Zhong, though."

"Okay," Jack said. "Have all his assets been frozen?"

"Yes, except for a few countries."

"What about children or mistresses?"

"We've questioned them extensively but have found nothing."

Jack pressed his lips together and took a deep breath. Not the news he wanted to hear. "Could they have been using a different WeChat account to communicate? With a different name? Or what about hidden SIM chips? Did you find any on them or in their car?"

The three generals exchanged a glance which told Jack all he needed to know—they hadn't even considered that.

Jack sighed, not quite sure why these seasoned government officials—both in China and the U.S.—were missing details that seemed clear as day to him.

"We understand that you have met Zhang Zhong," General Lin said. "Would you tell us exactly what transpired?"

Jack could recall the night quite clearly and relayed the whole story. "Zhang Zhong seems like the sort of person who holds grudges and will not give up easily. My guess is that we'll need to somehow lure him out."

"Do you have anything in mind?"

Jack frowned. "Where is Stanley Lin now?"

"He's in London, with his kids."

"Well, obviously Stanley communicates with Mr. Big. Maybe I can text Andrew, who I work with, and tell him I'll be visiting Shanghai and I'd like to meet up. I'll ask if Stanley can join. Then we'll see what happens." Jack paused. "Actually, it's probably best if I just text Andrew to say hello; the rest will follow naturally. But you'll need to give me some room so he doesn't get frightened away."

"That sounds risky," Wang Yang said.

It could be, but what other option was there? Jack didn't want to tell him that his faith in government officials—from either country—was faltering, and this meeting wasn't doing anything to help that. He shrugged, held his hands up. "That's the best idea I have. I want that guy buried in the ground." Now he looked right at Wang. "I found a bullet hole in my suitcase. If our luggage hadn't been in the trunk, it's entirely possible that Jojo or I might not be alive right now."

A pained expression crossed Wang's face. "Jack, I know you want to be involved, and it gives me great comfort knowing that you're protecting my daughter. But let us keep at it before you launch any plans. We'll look into your WeChat suggestion. That's a good one."

"Okay," Jack said reluctantly. "Make sure that the NSA helps you with the phone. My guess is that they used the SIM chip to turn on the phone, then logged into WeChat, sent messages, then logged out. They may have even deleted their messages. You'll need all the historical data to find out who they were communicating with. Then, you can track that person down. And if the NSA doesn't cooperate, please let me know."

Jack was reassured to see on their faces that they were familiar with the NSA; all three nodding as he made the suggestion.

The meeting wrapped up shortly after, and Liang escorted Jack back up and out to where Davis was waiting. As they made their way back to the hotel that Jack now called home, he knew he needed to be proactive in rooting out Zhang Zhong. He pulled his phone out of his pocket and thought about texting Andrew, even though he had told Wang and his generals that he would hold off. He didn't want to leave it up to the Chinese officials, or the American officials either. If they were able to find him, great, but Jack's gut told him that was wishful thinking.

And he would do whatever he had to do to ensure he and Jojo stayed safe.

CHAPTER 12

The next morning after breakfast, Jack went up to his office to work while Jojo saw a client about a sculpture commission. He sat down in one of the two swivel chairs and surveyed the space. He could look out the big picture windows and see the pool, a large rectangle bordered by tiles, its turquoise water shimmering like a gemstone. Beyond the tile and concrete of the pool were more trees; further beyond that towered the gate masked by the bamboo. It was calming and serene, a perfect way for his office to make him feel. He turned on his computer.

He drafted a note that he then typed into black phone to send to Cooper:

> *I would be grateful for your assistance with:*
>
> 1. *Arranging all six U.S./China trade representatives to meet next Thursday (or the following Thursday) for a 5pm meeting in Washington DC. A second meeting will be held the next day (Friday) at 10am in a W Hotel conference room.*
>
> 2. *Kindly ask the president if we can hold the first meeting in the president's private dining room. (Sandwiches, beer, salad, etc.). We would be honored if he could drop by to say hello. Meeting will last several hours.*
>
> 3. *I require two superior legal assistants who can type fast and have computers and printer. Preferably they would have solid international law backgrounds, with one having both China and America experience.*
>
> 4. *Inform both presidents to have ejection letters ready should I exercise my option to dismiss anyone. Also,*

> *ensure that they have a replacement individual within
> 10 minutes away so as to avoid delay.*
>
> 5. *Lastly, I need four Monopoly Board Games. One handy,
>   three sealed and discretely placed.*
>
> *Thank you.*

After he sent the message, he turned on his computer's VPN and went to Google News. Two headlines immediately caught his eye: *U.S. delays China tariffs for some items, including cellphones, removing other products from the list.* This was good news; it meant Sutton was trying to do some positive things to support the negotiations.

The second headline read: *China fixes its daily yuan midpoint—weaker than expected.* This, too, was a positive gesture, though none of them would have any impact on the negotiations.

His iPhone beeped and he reached over to pick it up. It was a text from Ari:

> *You just can't seem to stay out of the news. Great picture
> by the way. I heard what happened.*
>
> *Mary and I are in Beijing tonight and tomorrow night.
> You free for drinks? Joshua can join.*

Jack smiled. It would be good to see Ari; he hadn't seen him since the Control Center.

When he heard Jojo return, he closed his computer and went downstairs. He found her in the kitchen, making tea. "How'd it go?" he asked.

"It was good. Instead of another wife sculpture, as I was expecting, this is going to be a cat sculpture—a birthday present for his daughter."

"Well, I don't want to cut into any cat sculpture making time, but, I heard from Ari and he was asking if we'd like to get together for drinks tonight or tomorrow. His wife, Mary, will be there and it sounds like Joshua might, too."

"Yeah, tonight would be great. I don't think I've met Ari's wife."

"She does marketing for Nike. I think you two will get along. The last time I saw both of them was at a Shabbat dinner." A lifetime ago.

Jojo looked at him curiously. "What does 'Shabbat' mean?"

"It's a dinner Jewish people have on Friday nights. Ari is a member of the Synagogue Shanghai, and he asked me to go one night. If you're ever interested, maybe we could both go some time."

"I would love to do something like that. Sometimes, you still feel like a big mystery to me, Jack Gold."

He smiled. "Well, I'm not a practicing Jew or anything, but yeah, I bet you would enjoy yourself."

She put her teacup down and walked right up to him. "I always enjoy myself when I'm with you."

They kissed, and possibly would've continued the kiss if Mini hadn't started circling their legs, wagging his tail, yipping. Jack looked down.

"All right," he said. "Let's get you out for a walk."

*   *   *

That evening, they arrived at the Jianguo Hotel and found Ari, Mary, and Joshua sitting in the lobby, looking at their phones. Jack and Jojo stood there for a moment before Jack gave an exaggerated clearing of his throat. The three of them looked up.

"Hello, gentlemen," Jack said. "Hello, Mary. Are we interrupting anything?"

"Hey, guys," Joshua said.

"No, no interrupting," Ari said, slipping his phone in his pocket as he stood to shake Jack's hand. "Sorry if we seemed preoccupied." He turned to Jojo. "I swear, I'm not usually so rude. It's so nice to officially meet you; I remember you from Bar No. 3. I'm Ari."

Jojo smiled as she shook his hand. "I should've known the two of you were scheming something when I saw you guys at the bar."

"Well, don't blame Jack; I was the one who put the idea in his head."

Mary rolled her eyes. "Now, there you go trying to take all the credit. Jack, you did an incredible job, being put on the spot and having to talk to all those people."

Jack laughed. "Ari *does* have a point though—no way I'd have been involved in any of this if it wasn't for him."

They went into the bar and got a table, ordered a round of drinks.

"You know what we were watching?" Mary said. "On our phones?"

Jack shook his head. "No, what?"

"The video."

He paused, waiting for her to elaborate, but she didn't. "The video? I'm afraid you're going to have to refresh my memory."

"It's nothing you haven't seen before," Ari said. "Or, more accurately, you're the star of the show, so I'm sure you remember it."

"Oh," Jack said. "*That* video."

Mary grinned. "Yes, *that* video." She looked at Jojo. "Have you seen this video yet?"

"I don't think I have," Jojo said, glancing at Jack.

Mary scooted her chair a little closer to Jojo and held their phone between the two of them. "You'd definitely remember it if you saw it."

Their drinks arrived, and Jack happily took a big sip of his beer while Jojo watched the video of him throwing those two guys off the balcony. She smiled after Mary put the phone down.

"That was impressive," she said, "though not as impressive as what he did to those three guys the other day."

Jack remembered being assaulted by the two Chinese that night because he was an American. He had asked them to stop, but they didn't. Neither Mary or Jojo seemed alarmed that people would think that way. If a Chinese person were attacked in America it would be all over the news in China. There would be outrage.

Ari leaned toward Jack. "So, after your little shootout, I received a call from Israel's president's office. They *really* want you to visit. It's only a nine-hour flight."

"I haven't forgotten," Jack said. "I'd like Jojo to go too."

"That shouldn't be a problem."

"I'll be going back to Washington next week to discuss the trade negotiations. I'm hoping it goes smoothly and I won't get held up there any longer than necessary." He looked at Jojo. "Interested in going to Israel?"

She grinned. "I would love to!"

Jack returned her smile. "Guess you'll be putting that passport to good use." He looked at Ari. "Let's plan on figuring out something when I get back. But Jojo and I would be honored to make that trip."

He took a sip of his drink and glanced at Jojo, who was laughing over something Mary had just said. Sometimes, it was hard to believe the sequence of events that had transpired to get him here, but he was beyond grateful that Jojo was a part of his life, that they were on this adventure together.

CHAPTER 13

Back in Washington the following week, Jack tried to keep focused on the trade negotiations but found his thoughts kept slipping back to Mr. Big. He hadn't been given any updates, other than they still had no idea where Mr. Big was. Being away from Jojo was hard, though he took comfort in knowing their place was secure, and that he would be back with her in a few days.

When he arrived at the White House, the two attorneys were already there, waiting.

Rebecca was tall, with blue eyes, a blond haired ponytail, and a firm handshake.

"Nice to meet you," she said. "I went to Harvard Law, I interned with Roberts, and I now work at Cravath, Swaine & Moore, mostly doing international corporate work."

"Great," Jack said. "Appreciate you being here."

The second person was a large Chinese man named Eric. "I'm an American," he said, "but I grew up in China and then went to Northwestern, then Yale Law. I work in Beijing with Wachtell, mainly assisting large corporations on domestic and international transactions."

"Excellent," Jack said. "I'm glad to have you both. Today will be less formal than the meeting tomorrow. However, I'm hoping to have people sign a few documents today. You'll know what I'll need as we go through things. Let's make sure whatever they sign is enforceable in America *and* China. If you spot a problem, notify me immediately. Your job is to keep me out of trouble. Other than that, no need to take meeting notes. Just note the key issues."

Rebecca and Eric nodded.

"Have you seen the agreement Wang and Sutton signed?"

"I have not," Rebecca replied, and Eric shook his head.

Jack went over to the conference table, where he had left his brief-case. Four sets of Monopoly sat in the center of the table, which he moved to a side table by the far wall. He'd get to the board games later. He opened his briefcase and took out his laptop. "Why don't you two come over here and read it," he said, pulling the file up. "That's the framework within which we'll be operating."

When they finished reading, Rebecca looked up. "Did you write this, Mr. Gold?"

"Please, call me Jack. And yes, I did. Did you find any mistakes?"

"No. It's well written. It empowers the people coming today and requires compliance by both presidents." Eric was nodding as she spoke. "Nice work."

"Thanks," Jack said. "Why don't you get started on writing up the nondisclosure agreement. We'll need copies for myself, the six delegates and their translators, and you two."

"I'm on it," Rebecca said as the door opened people began to file in. It was the Chinese delegation first, followed a few minutes later by the Americans. Both sides had an interpreter with them.

Jack introduced himself and his two assistants, and then gestured to the far wall where a table had been laid with an assortment of sand-wiches and salad and fruit.

"Help yourself," he said, "or, if you'd prefer to wait until later, that's fine, too."

"We can wait," one of the Chinese delegates said through the inter-preter. Everyone took their seats; the three Americans sat on one side with their interpreter, the three Chinese on the other with their inter-preter. Jack sat at the head. Rebecca and Eric were seated behind Jack, laptops open on their laps.

Jack took a deep breath. "Hello, everyone," he said. "Since we're in America, I will speak English. When we're in China, I'll speak Chinese." He paused to let the translator do his work. "Today, I'd like to do just a few easy things. But first, I'd like everyone to introduce themselves, and maybe let us know a little bit about your background and relevant experience."

"I'm Chris," the first American said, a middle-aged man with thinning brown hair and wire rimmed glasses. "I have a background in negotia-tions and teach at Georgetown University. I've settled many union labor disputes, so I'm hopeful that I'll be able to help out here."

The man next to him, Tom, was from China but had been an American citizen for a decade now. "I have a PhD in economics from Stanford, and I'm a fellow at the Hoover Institution." Jack nodded, pleased. The Hoover Institution was a bastion of free market thinking and attracted only the best and the brightest from around the world. Jack was relieved there was a solid, educated mind on the American side.

Seated next to Tom was Jennifer, who had a PhD in international business from Princeton University and currently worked in the Department of Commerce.

They continued to go through with the introductions. The Chinese had brought a senior bank CEO and Bank of China board member named Gui, who graduated from Tsinghua University, a woman named Xia with a PhD in economics and currently a professor at Jiaotong University, and a young man named Jiang, with a master's in economics who worked in China's Ministry of Commerce.

"Thank you, everyone," Jack said, once the introductions were done. He felt good about this group—they were intelligent, experienced people. There would likely be some disagreements, but he was confident they would be able to resolve them, so long as everyone remained respectful and open.

"So," Jack said. "Our goal is to come to an agreement that benefits the people of China and America. There's lots of political bickering and posturing going on right now and I'd like to separate ourselves from that." Everyone nodded. "One of the biggest challenges this group faces," Jack continued, "is constantly being influenced by outside people and information. An agreement hasn't worked out in the past just for this reason. That's why I developed a framework enabling us to make decisions here that would then be enforced. Which is why all of you are here."

As he spoke, he made eye contact with each person. "For us to work together, we must have confidentiality. In other words, this should be a safe place for anyone to say anything, without fear of reprisal later." Everyone, except Gui, the senior bank official, nodded, which didn't entirely surprise Jack; all bank board members were senior party members. "After we sign this, should anyone disclose information we discuss, they will receive a one-hundred-thousand dollar fine, which can be increased by a majority vote of this group, the seven of us."

Jack waited while Rebecca and Eric distributed freshly printed copies of the nondisclosure agreement. "The attorneys and translators will also sign this."

There was the sound of papers being shuffled as everyone looked through the NDA. Jack watched Gui, who was glaring at the papers. He muttered, "*Bèndàn de wàigúorén.*"

Jack took out his black phone and, underneath the table, typed: *Eject the Bank of China man. Bring his replacement.*

He slipped the phone back into his pocket and looked at the translator. "Please translate what I'm about to say." Then he looked at Gui, and, speaking in Chinese said, "You just called me a stupid foreigner. Which was not only rude, but also incorrect. *You* are the foreigner in America. And now you're dismissed."

Gui's eyes narrowed as his face turned crimson. "You cannot dismiss me," he sputtered. "The president of China appointed me."

"He may have appointed you, but he gave me the authority to remove you."

The door opened and a woman, flanked by two security officials, came in. She had the letter from Wang, stating the authority he was granting Jack for the trade negotiations. Gui read it, his expression of rage growing.

He threw the piece of paper down and yanked his briefcase off the floor. He glared at Jack, seemed about to say something, but then wisely thought twice before he was escorted out by the Secret Service agents. Jack remained seated, exterior calm. He looked around the room.

"Jack," Chris said, glancing to the door. "You can't just kick someone out like that. I've done lots of negotiations; let me help you."

Jack looked at him. "Give me three examples of subsidies that come from the U.S. government or local states."

Chris opened his mouth but then closed it. A frown appeared. "Uh, well, let's see . . ."

Jack gave him a few moments but knew that he wouldn't be able to come up with anything. There was no reason to prolong this. Jack discreetly sent a second text message on his phone, and Chris was likewise escorted from the room, though he was more baffled than angry.

"Okay," Jack said, once the door had closed. "They'll be sending their replacements in shortly. While we wait for that, why don't we get something to eat." He gestured to the table with food, and then sat back in his chair when the others went up to get something to eat. He was glad the theatrics were over, though he could tell by the quiet in the room that everyone else was surprised two people had been removed. Jack stood up and selected himself a pastrami sandwich and a Diet Coke.

When the replacements came in, Jack was surprised to see that he recognized the American; it took him a minute but then he realized they had met at the Shabbat dinner in Shanghai.

"Sean Smith," he said, holding his hand out. "Assistant Consul General for the U.S. Embassy in Shanghai."

Jack smiled as he shook his hand. "Yes, we met at the Synagogue Shanghai."

"Ah, good memory. We did. Good to see you again."

The Chinese man was warmly greeted by the other two Chinese, who were clearly much happier to be working with him than Gui. His name was Li, and he was an investor in both American and Chinese high-tech companies.

After both men had signed the NDAs, Jack went over what they would be going through tomorrow. "I have a list I'll give you so prior to the meeting, you can select what you think are the three most important issues." He steepled his fingers. "What we agree on will become a formal trade agreement, so we need to make sure that we're all on the same page. If any issue is not fully agreed upon, it won't become part of the overall trade agreement."

Li leaned forward, looking at Jack. "What constitutes an agreement?"

"Well," Jack said. "My suggestion would be a simple majority. There are seven people here."

"But there are four Americans," Li said. "And only three Chinese."

"It may appear that way," Jack replied. "But—and you're just going to have to trust me on this—I am not in favor of one side more than the other, and I cannot stress this enough. I am interested in seeing both countries equally benefit from this trade negotiation."

"May we have a moment to discuss this?"

"Of course."

While they huddled at the far end of the room, Tom, seated to Jack's left, leaned over. "They're never going to agree to that," he whispered.

Jack took a sip of his soda, watching the group. He hoped that wouldn't be the case.

He was pleasantly surprised when, after the Chinese returned to the table, he asked for a show of hands indicating how many people were in favor of a majority vote, and everyone's hand went up. When he looked at Li, the man gave him the briefest of nods and a smile, which Jack knew was meant to convey the fact that yes, the people of China did trust that he had their best interest in mind. He had gone to great lengths to prove it, after all.

The attorneys handed out another round of paperwork for everyone to sign, affirming their agreement, and then the meeting was technically over.

"But before you leave," Jack said, "I'd like to ask that we play a game together. I want you to pick a partner from the other side; we'll be playing in teams."

"Ah," Tom said, glancing at the side table where the games sat. "I was wondering what that was for."

Jack opened the game and while the teams picked out their game piece, he set up the money, cards, and properties.

The game started. Jack paid close attention to see how the teams would play, how they would ultimately make their decisions. He also played, though he didn't have a partner, which made the decision-making far easier. The game went on for a while, until there were only a few properties not yet purchased. No one had all the properties of any one color. Finally, when it was Jack's turn, he looked at Tom and Li.

"If you give me Pacific Avenue, I'll give you half the rent when people land on it and I'll let you land on it for free."

Tom and Li looked at each other and then nodded. "Might be the only way we make any money," Tom said wryly.

Jack rolled double fours and landed on one of his own properties. He picked up the dice, getting to go a second time since he'd gotten doubles. But before taking his turn, he turned to Sean and Xia and convinced them to agree to a similar trade as Tom and Li. "I'm going to buy six houses for the green and put that money in the bank; I'm also going to buy four houses for the orange." He placed the houses only on the properties he owned and then waited for the outcry.

"That's not fair!" they all exclaimed. "You have to distribute the houses equally," Tom added.

"Actually," Jack said, "the rules allow the owner to place houses unevenly."

No one spoke for a moment as they all looked at the board, varying degrees of perplexity on their faces. Jack had tricked them, though it was a trick they had agreed to. The game continued, and despite Jack ending up in jail several times, he was still able to collect a substantial amount of money as the players landed on his various properties.

When the game finally ended, no one was surprised that Jack had won. He stood up, stretching, feeling several vertebrate in his spine crack now that he was no longer sitting.

"Good game everyone," he said. "I'm wondering if I could speak to Sean, Jennifer, and Tom for a moment?"

The three Americans went over to Jack and formed a circle. "There are three sets of Monopoly on the side table over there," Jack said in a low voice. "I think it would be nice if you gave your partner one, and, if you enjoyed the game this evening and getting to know them, let them know."

Sean glanced over his shoulder at the side table. "I was wondering what the extra sets were for," he said. "That's a great idea."

Jack could see the Chinese were delighted by the gift; despite losing the game, they had seemed to enjoy the evening, and, Jack hoped, would remember it.

*   *   *

Their meeting the following morning started at ten sharp. Jack was pleased that everyone managed to arrive a few minutes early, so they were able to start right on time.

Jack took a sip of his coffee and set the cup down. Everyone else had their own cup of coffee or tea in front of them as well. "Before we start talking about each of your top issues, I wanted to make a proposal. If we can come to an *approved* vote regarding all of the items, then we agree to immediately lift all sanctions. There are more than six major issues. But, if we can tackle the six, that means we've come a long way and should try to ease some pain in the markets. Tariffs are hurting both countries." Everyone nodded. "If someone wants to reinstall them later, they can call for a vote at any time."

He took another sip of his coffee while he let the proposal sink in.

"Those in favor?" Jack asked.

Six hands went up.

"Good." He waited while Rebecca and Eric distributed the resolution paperwork for everyone to sign. Then, it was time to move on to the top issues.

On the American side, the issues ranged from China subsidizing companies to currency manipulation; for the Chinese it was having free access to invest in and connect to American financial institutions and protection from the American government restricting products based on false security-related issues.

Rebecca and Eric stood on either side of the white board, Rebecca writing down the list of American concerns, Eric writing down the list of Chinese concerns.

"The first item on the American side," Jack said. "The Chinese government should not be allowed to subsidize companies and industries like steel. Okay. But, have you considered that America does the same thing?"

Jennifer and Tom looked at each other, shaking their heads. "What do you mean?" Tom asked.

"Well, like getting a tax credit if you buy an electric car. Or states giving out rebates for installing solar panels."

"That's different," Jennifer said. "The Chinese subsidies enable Chinese companies to produce steel below cost, in effect wiping out the steel industry in America."

"Do you believe in free markets?"

"Of course."

"Do you think Milton Friedman was an excellent economist?"

Jennifer nodded. "Of course I do. I share nearly all of his viewpoints."

"Great." Jack looked around the room as he opened his laptop. "I've brought Dr. Friedman here today to share some of his wisdom." The video was already up, so Jack waited while everyone gathered around and then clicked play. The Nobel laureate began to speak on the YouTube video.

"Let us suppose that the Japanese flooded us with steel, that will reduce employment in the steel industry. However, it will increase employment elsewhere. We will pay for the steel with dollars. What are the Japanese going to do with the dollars they got for the steel? They are not going to burn them. They are not going to tear them up. That would be best of all. Because there is nothing we can produce more cheaply than green pieces of paper. And, if they were willing to send us steel to just take back green

pieces of paper I can think of no better deal. The dollars they spend will eventually find their way back to the United States as demand for goods and services. You will have less employment in the steel industry and more employment in the industry producing the goods we export. Overall total employment will not be affected. But overall the American consumer will benefit because he will get the steel more cheaply and the goods made from steel more cheaply than he otherwise would. That's the benefit to the American consumer."

Jack closed the laptop and looked at the three Americans. "Can we remove that issue from the list?" They nodded.

They continued on through each item written on the whiteboard. Jack listened to everyone's varying viewpoints, and would offer his own when he felt necessary. He then made a proposition he hoped everyone would agree to.

His proposition consisted of five parts. "China will agree to make all its banks and state-owned enterprises public within the next eighteen months. The government can only retain a twenty-five percent stake; sensitive security and military-related companies are exempt.

"Second, Chinese companies will be treated like local companies within the U.S. while also having the right to integrate into America's financial system directly for payment mechanisms, like Alipay. If a presidential order is required, it will be given," he added, seeing a frown cross Li's face.

"Third, America will no longer call China a currency regulator. Fourth, China will agree to treat American companies the same as local companies." He paused and let the words sink in. "There will be no favoritism in the private sector. Imports to and from both countries will be treated as if they were local. In other words, if China inspects beef from America, it must also inspect its local beef. It will be a level playing field. America will have the right to invest and operate in industries that had previously been limited. And fifth—neither country will restrict the selling and buying of products unless laws have been broken. Now, this will need to be fine-tuned by the attorneys, but you get the picture."

They took a thirty-minute lunch break, which Jack hoped would give everyone time to think about what he had just laid out, as well as allow Rebecca and Eric enough time to type up, from his notes, a formal proposal.

When they reconvened, the topic of IP came up. "China has been stealing American IP for years," Tom said. "The courts have been slow to enforce, there is favoritism to locals, and the penalties have been low or nonexistent."

"But it's improving," Li said. "It's getting better and better. Plus, Chinese firms do care about having their IP protected."

Sean shook his head. "We have a problem with the national security imminent threat provision. With Heidan's 5G equipment, you can't tell. There may be a hardware or software risk, which can change when they upload enhancements."

"Okay," Jack said. "You bring up a good point. What if we add another clause? Something along the lines of, *If a company has been known to breach its security-related promises elsewhere, or the product has been nefariously used, the product can be rightly be restricted.*" Heidan, Jack knew, had done exactly that in Africa.

"That's sufficient," Sean said.

The conversation went back and forth for several minutes, which Jack had expected; China would never accept an outside authority controlling their patent office. But something had to be done.

"What about this," Jack said. "Anyone can appeal an IP case to this body if they disagree with the ruling, or if it's taking too long, or the penalty paid falls materially short of international norms. If the court is overruled, they pay all of our fees. We may engage an outside thirty-party firm or individual to assist us in making rulings. We could use this enforcement mechanism for all aspects of this agreement."

Tom looked up from the notes he was scribbling on his legal pad. "How will we have money to operate?"

"Each government will put twenty-five billion in an escrow account in Switzerland. This group can use those funds for our operational costs and, if necessary, at its majority vote to compensate harmed parties as a means of an enforcement mechanism. The group will continue in perpetuity. Countries can replace their delegates at any time. My position can be removed upon the unanimous agreement of the president of China and the president of the United States."

"I think twenty-five billion is low," Tom said. Li and Xia nodded.

"Okay," Jack said. "How about fifty billion?"

No one objected, knowing full well that if there was not money at stake, no action would ever be taken.

The discussion continued until everyone seemed satisfied with where they were. The Chinese had done their best to keep Heidan safe and the Americans seemed happy with the direction things were going to remedy China's IP stealing. Eric and Rebecca wrote up the formal agreement for everyone to sign. The attorneys had formalized the language, making it compulsory for each country and the presidents. Jack was handed the original and then draft copies were made so everyone would have their own. After everyone reviewed the final language, Jack circulated his copy for signature.

The mood in the room was positive, and Jack felt encouraged that things had gone relatively smoothly. "We just have one more item to sign," he said, "before we're done. It's the formal communication to both presidents regarding lifting tariffs. It should be worded something along the lines of 'There is unanimous agreement that trade tariffs must immediately be eliminated. More trade-related information to come.'"

Rebecca's fingers skittered across the laptop keys. She printed one copy for everyone to circulate and read over. With no objections, Jack's copy was signed. He added his signature last, and then took out his black phone and snapped a photo of the one-page document. He sent it to Cooper, with a simple directive: *Please circulate*. This way, it would get to both Sutton and Wang. China, Jack new, would be pleased.

That done, he took a deep breath and looked around the room, again noting the relaxed, friendly atmosphere. This was good. "Not to sound too self-congratulatory, but I think we've done a remarkable job. It's a done deal. But there are still things we should discuss, like sales of fentanyl, cybersecurity, and other ways to enhance trade. So, I look forward to meeting in Beijing. My guess is that a number of you will be pressured to disclose what transpired during your visit, but I urge you to not reveal anything. It'd be best if you were not influenced by others until we finish. But for now—I think we can call it a day." He had considered having a dinner for all of them, but decided against it, not wanting it to be seen as a celebration. Even though it *was* something to be celebrated.

He put the signed documents into a manila envelope and then slipped it into his briefcase. He'd pass the envelope on to Davis.

As he was saying his goodbyes, his iPhone beeped. After he exited the room, he pulled his phone out and read the message from Gerard, at Harry Winston: *Mr. Gold, your ring is ready whenever you'd like to stop by.*

Jack smiled as he slipped the phone back into his pocket. He couldn't wait to see the ring, but more than that, he couldn't wait to get back to Jojo. He spotted Davis and went over, gave him the manila envelope.

"For safe keeping, please," he said. "And I'd like to depart for Beijing as soon as possible."

Davis took the envelope. "Absolutely."

"I'll need to make one stop when we land in Beijing, if we could."

"Oh?"

"Harry Winston. I need to pick something up."

Normally stoic Davis let a rare smile of congratulations cross his face. "Nice," he said. "Well, we'll definitely make sure to do that."

Jack took his phone out and texted Gerard back and let him know he would be there to pick up the ring the following morning.

CHAPTER 14

The ring was stunning and had come out better than Jack had imagined. The black band and the red of the diamond contrasted beautifully, and instead of merely securing the diamond to the band, the six black prongs appeared to be gently hugging it. It was a beautiful ring, and he could already envision Jojo wearing it.

The problem was—he couldn't quite conjure up *how* he was going to propose. He couldn't see himself organizing some magical, orchestrated moment. No, that wasn't his way at all, and if he tried to force something, it would come out inauthentic. He hoped he'd just know when the right time was. He tried to dismiss his nervousness, but . . . What if she said no?

He had the ring in his pocket, in its black velvet box, but it bulged and the outline was clearly visible. She'd probably notice it right away and then he'd be forced to either lie or ask her right then and there. He took the box out and removed the ring, slipped it deep back into his pocket, and put the box in his briefcase. He would ask her today—he couldn't bear to have this anxiety about not knowing her answer—he just wasn't sure exactly when. Or how.

Davis gave Jack a smile and a pat on the shoulder after he dropped him off, stopping short of saying "Good luck," which Jack appreciated. His nerves over this were bad enough.

"Hello?" he called as he walked inside. Mini came racing over to him, and Jack leaned down to greet the dog.

"Is that you?" Jojo's voice rang out from the back of the room, in her workspace. "I'm working. My hands are all dirty."

Jack left his bags and went and found Jojo, who was in jeans and a button-down white shirt with the sleeves rolled up, her hands and forearms streaked with clay. Her hair was up in a bun, a pencil securing it.

"I can still give you a kiss," he said, leaning down to do just that.

"How'd it go?"

"Pretty well, actually," he said. "I'm happy with the progress we made, and the people on both sides are good people." Jack stifled a huge yawn that muscled its way through. "I might drag that sofa over here so I can be near you while you work, if you don't mind. Feeling a little jet-lagged."

"Yeah, of course."

He dragged the sofa from their living area over near Jojo, where there was plenty of space for both the couch and for her to continue working. Jack kicked his shoes off and stretched out, fluffed the pillow under his head.

He yawned again. "Babe, I'm so tired. But I want to hear about what you've been up to. How have you been?"

"Oh, good," she said, going back to work on a piece of clay that, at least to Jack's eye, hadn't quite taken form of anything recognizable yet. "Mini kept me company and we took some nice walks. And then I had dinner with my dad and . . ."

He told himself he was going to rest his eyelids while Jojo filled him in, but the soothing sound of her voice lulled him to sleep before she was able to finish her third sentence.

Jack wasn't sure how much time had passed when he finally reopened his eyes, but he was still there, on the sofa, and Jojo was still there, facing him as she worked, though it looked to be different than the piece she had been working on earlier.

He stretched and sat up. Jojo stopped what she was doing and looked over at him with a smile.

"Have a good nap?" she asked.

"How long was I asleep for?"

She shrugged. "A few hours? You looked so peaceful. Want to see?"

He looked at her, confused. "Huh?"

"Come here."

He stood up and went over and knelt down next to her. She had sculpted him, asleep on the sofa. Stretched out on his left side, his eyes closed, a serene expression on his face.

"Wow," he said. "I look that relaxed when I sleep? I had no idea." He slipped his hand into his pocket, his fingers closing around the ring. "Jojo . . ." They were both kneeling, but what did that matter? "Baby, I've been thinking for a long time about us, and the future. And when I think about the future, I can't imagine one without you in it." He pulled the ring from his pocket, picked it up from the palm of his hand, and held it out to her. "Nothing would make me happier than to always be with you. Will you marry me?"

Her dark eyes went from the ring, to his face, then back to the ring, a slight frown and a slight smile simultaneously happening on her face. "What is that?" she said. "What did you say?"

"Well . . . this is a red diamond. In a Tungsten setting. And . . . I'm really hoping you'll want to marry me." His insides twisted. Shouldn't she have just said yes and jumped into his arms?

"It's gorgeous." Her brow smoothed and she grinned. "Yes, Jack Gold, nothing would make me happier than to marry you."

Joy and relief flooded him—he pulled her to him for a hug before he slipped the ringer on her finger. It fit perfectly and looked even more stunning on her hand, streaked with clay and everything.

"Wow, Jack," she said, holding her hand up to look at the ring. "You got this for me?"

"Just for you."

She turned her hand to admire the diamond from both sides. "This isn't your typical engagement ring. I don't think I've ever seen such a beautiful ring before. It's so unique."

"You deserve it. You deserve so much more than that, but now since you've agreed to marry me, I have the rest of our lives together to work on that." He smiled. "The band is made of Tungsten, which is very strong. And as you can see there, it has six prongs so you can wear it while you work and not have to worry."

Tears came to her eyes. "This ring is like a representation of your love and my art. You've somehow managed to express my art in the form of a ring. I would never have imagined something like this. It's so beautiful."

"It is," he said. "And if you ever decide to wash your hands, we'll be able to see how it looks properly."

She looked at him with a mischievous smile and then put her hands on either side of his face, pulling him in for a kiss. "There," she said when they pulled apart. "Now you need a shower too."

When they were done in the shower, Jack felt refreshed and invigorated. Now that Jojo's hands were clean, he took a few photos of her with the ring.

"You should send one to my dad," Jojo said. "He'll be thrilled. Actually, let me do it."

She grabbed her phone and took a photo of just her hand and then began typing a message. "*Great news,*" she read aloud as she typed. "*Your daughter is engaged to a Mr. Jack Gold. Do you approve?*"

Jack picked the best photo from the selection he had taken and sent a few messages himself, to his own father, to Paul, to Ari and Joshua. *We're engaged,* he wrote, marveling at the fact that he was actually typing those words.

"My dad is going to be so happy," Jojo said. "He likes you a lot. I think he was hoping this would happen sooner rather than later." Her phone began to ring. "Oh, it's my dad."

Though he couldn't understand the Suzhou dialect Jojo spoke with her father, Jack listened to her laughter and happy exclamations, and it sounded, to him, as if Wang shared in her excitement.

She looked at Jack when she hung up the phone. "My father is thrilled—he hasn't sounded that happy in years. He'd like us to drop by and say hello and see the ring and talk about our plans at some point. Though he's not trying to rush us into anything," she added.

"Sounds great."

"Okay, now you're going to have to excuse me for a few minutes while I get in touch with some of my other friends—they're going to die when they see this ring!"

Jack couldn't help but smile—she had said yes to marrying him and she loved the ring. And just seeing her happy and excited to share this news made him feel like the luckiest man alive.

CHAPTER 15

The trade negotiation meeting in China was held at Jade Spring Mountain, where all the produce was grown for the leadership. Jack had never been there before and was excited to get to see it. He was also interested in getting a glimpse of the well-trained Central Security Bureau that guarded the area.

The first thing he saw when they arrived were hangars and barracks. Davis pulled up to the compound and a tall Chinese woman came out; she was young, with a short, wavy haircut, probably in her twenties, Jack guessed. She was stylishly dressed in bright colors and approached Jack with a friendly smile.

"Hello, Mr. Gold," she said. "My name is Meifeng. Welcome to Jade Spring Mountain. Let me show you to your room."

Jack grabbed his briefcase and his suitcase, bid goodbye to Davis, and followed Meifeng toward one of the barracks.

"Most of the produce for China's leadership is grown here," she said. Jack nodded, taking in the view beyond the buildings. It was a picture of beautiful symmetry, rows and rows of green as far as the eye could see. To his left spanned vast orchards of fruit trees—persimmon, Mandarin orange, Asian pear, plum. There were guards stationed here and there, but even with their presence, the bucolic nature of the place made even them seem serene.

"Here's your room, Mr. Gold," Meifeng said. They had stopped in front of one of the barracks. She handed him a key. "I'll be back at four forty-five to escort you to the meeting. You have a little time now to relax and explore, if you'd like."

"Thank you," Jack said, taking the key. He let himself in. It was simple and clean—concrete floor, atop which sat a bed, a sofa, a wingback chair, and then a desk with swivel chair. The one modern touch was a large flat-screen TV mounted to the wall.

Jack put his briefcase and luggage down and stretched, trying to ease the tightness that had crept into his lower back muscles. He did some stretches and a bunch of pushups, and then went out for a walk.

What a peaceful place, he thought. He could see all the way down the mountain into the valley. He took a deep breath, filling his lungs with the fresh mountain air. He walked past the barracks toward the hangars. The first one he passed by had been converted into offices; he peeked in an open window and saw several people inside, sitting at desks, hard at work. He continued on. The second hangar was bustling with action; workers were standing at long tables packaging freshly harvested produce. The third hangar was empty, except for a large conference table bordered by empty chairs and a smaller table close by.

Jack turned and started to head back to the barracks. He'd rest for a little while and then get ready for the meeting. He had a good feeling about it, though, as if holding it at this beautiful location was a sign that the negotiations would go smoothly.

*   *   *

At four forty-five, Meifeng returned and escorted Jack to the meeting, in the third hangar he had passed by earlier. People were filing in and taking their seats; Jack greeted everyone as he set his briefcase down. Rebecca and Eric had a desk of their own set up right near where Jack would be sitting.

"How are you guys doing?" he asked.

"Good," Rebecca said. "Just trying to make sure both of these printers are connected."

"Okay, great. I'll be needing your help today, as usual."

"That's what we're here for," Eric said with a smile. "This place is pretty cool."

Jack went over to a side table that was set up with tea and light refreshments. He poured himself a cup and then took his seat.

Once everyone else was seated, he began. "It's good to see everyone again," he said. "We have a number of things to accomplish today. Just to give you a brief overview, we'll be dealing with Fentanyl, cybersecurity–"

Before he was able to complete the sentence, the door opened and a man strode in. He was tall with a medium build and muscular physique.

Jack recognized him as he approached; it was Ren Yao, the president of Heidan.

Jack slipped his phone out of his pocket and, underneath the table, tapped the code to unlock it. He stood up and turned slightly toward Eric, who was seated behind him at the desk. He discreetly handed him the phone. "I want you to subtly video record this entire exchange."

Eric took the phone and Jack turned back, looked at the three Chinese delegates. "Who violated their nondisclosure agreement?"

"I know who it was," Ren said, before anyone could answer. "And I will pay all the related fees and penalties."

"Sir," Jack said, "you are not invited to attend the China American trade talks. You shouldn't be here."

Ren held up his hands. "I just wanted to give you some background. Don't you think it's of utmost importance to be fully informed when discussing important matters such as these?"

"I propose we increase the financial penalty to ten million." Jack raised his hand. All but one sitting at the table also did.

Ren did not appear bothered. "The 5G software and hardware are secure. What I don't think you understand is–"

"You should be talking to the United States–not us," Jack said. "I propose raising the penalty to thirty million." He raised his hand. Same vote as last time.

Now Ren looked a little exasperated, but not deterred. Pocket change for him, Jack knew. But still.

"We can work out an arrangement where the U.S. is in full control," Ren said.

"Fifty million." Hands raised.

Ren rolled his eyes. "I'm not paying fifty million." He walked over and stood right in front of Jack. This close, Jack could see the rage filling his eyes, the way the muscle in his jaw quivered. "I have a better idea–" As he spoke, he lunged out with his right arm, shoving Jack's head back with such force that Jack's feet flew out from under him and he landed heavily on the floor.

He stayed there for a moment–not hurt, just shocked. But then the shock dissipated and adrenaline and anger flooded him. He jumped up. "You just assaulted an American diplomat."

Ren gave a short, barking laugh. "You think *that* was an assault?"

But Jack was ready this time, and as Ren swung his arm around, this time with a closed fist, Jack launched a front kick right into Ren's stomach, simultaneously sweeping the punch away with his right hand. Doing so Ren's right ribs were unprotected, and Jack swiftly landed two solid punches. He stepped back as Ren staggered in front of him, clutching his torso.

Jack held both hands up. "I don't want to fight you. Let's just—"

"Fuck America, fuck Americans, *CàoNǐMa*!" Ren kicked out his right leg, but Jack was ready and caught his leg with both arms. Jack pivoted so his back was to Ren and unleashed a back kick to his groin. Jack then grabbed Ren's left arm and lifted, allowing him to again attack his exposed rib cage. He delivered several excruciating punches, heard the cartilage and likely several ribs cracking. Ren doubled over but didn't fall.

"Fuck America," he said, a string of saliva dangling from his lower lip.

Jack put two hands in a karate pose in front of him and lowered himself into a karate stance. Anchored to the ground, he twisted his entire upper body around, lashing out with an extended right leg, delivering a devastating spinning back kick right to Ren's head. He fell to the ground as Jack landed solidly back in the pose he had started.

The room was silent.

Jack let out a breath and walked over to Eric, who was staring at him, wide eyed. "You can stop recording," Jack said.

Eric nodded wordlessly and handed the phone back to Jack. He then selected the video and forwarded it to Cooper, with the message: *Circulate to Wang, Sutton, and news outlets.*

The door opened again and Meifeng appeared. "Is everything all right?" she asked. She looked at Jack, who was still holding his phone. "Mr. Gold, I'm sorry, cell phones don't work in here."

"Mine does just fine," Jack looked to the others. "I just sent President Wang and President Sutton that entire exchange." He turned to Meifeng. "It's time to let in the American Embassy staff to interview everyone."

Meifeng widened her eyes. "Oh, that's not possible. No other foreigners are authorized to enter this facility."

Jack shook his head. "Sorry. I know you need to follow your rules, but an American diplomat was just assaulted. This after nearly being murdered by three Chinese. I demand to know who let that man enter this facility. Let the American Embassy staff in here immediately. Plus, he needs medical attention."

Without saying anything, the three Chinese delegates stood up and exited the hangar. Meifeng followed. Jack looked at Ren, who was still on the ground, now clutching his head and groaning.

"Well," Jack said. He went over to the refreshments table and selected a Diet Coke. When he sat back down, the remaining three Americans at the table still had expressions of utter shock on their faces. "I'd say negotiations are proceeding nicely, wouldn't you?" Jack cracked open the soda and took a sip.

It was unfathomable that someone would enter uninvited like that, and then to have that sort of fight ensue . . . Jack turned around to look at Rebecca and Eric. "I think we should prepare something to sign confirming Ren's agreement to pay the penalty. We'll need to issue him a formal request for funds and provide him wire transfer details."

"Got it," Rebecca said. Eric only nodded, still looking at Jack in disbelief.

"Now," Jack said, turning back to the table. "Are you okay with staying here, or would you prefer to relocate to a different hotel for tonight and tomorrow?"

"Relocate," came the reply from all three, in near perfect unison.

"Would it be . . . would it be all right if we stayed elsewhere, too?" Eric asked.

"Absolutely," Jack said.

The door flew open and Davis strode into the room, glancing at Ren Yao as he walked past. "What happened?"

Jack handed him the phone and let him watch the video.

"We're leaving," Davis said the second the video finished. He tossed a disgusted look in Ren's direction. "He assaulted an American diplomat. The military let him in. We're leaving now. We'll submit a formal complaint along with this video, but we'll do that later. Get your things."

"I'd like the trade talks to continue tomorrow. And we'll need to arrange transport for these three and the two attorneys to a hotel in Beijing. Is that possible?"

"Yes," Davis said. He looked at the three delegates. "I'm with the American Embassy. We'll give you a ride and the two attorneys can go with Jackson. So gather your things, everyone; we're leaving."

Jack started to get his things together too. "Who's seen the video?" Davis asked.

"I sent it to Cooper and told him to pass it on to Wang, Sutton, and the news outlets."

"Smart," Davis said. "You'll never have to buy a drink in an American bar again."

There was more commotion at the door as a group of Chinese men walked in, followed by a medical unit. The medical unit went to attend Ren; the group of men came over to confront Jack.

"Did you hurt that man?" one of the men asked.

"Did you let him into this facility?" Jack demanded. "I'd like to find that out first."

"Actually," Davis said, "we're leaving."

"You are going nowhere," the man said.

"Why don't you watch this and then see if your assessment of the situation has changed." Jack held his phone out and pressed play.

There wasn't much to argue with after seeing the video, so once Jack had his things, he followed Davis out of the hangar. The three Chinese delegates were standing nearby, looking as if they weren't sure whether they should stay or go. Jack walked over to them. "The Americans would rather stay someplace else. Can you arrange something in Beijing, something nice? We're leaving now, but just let me know via WeChat where to go."

"Yes," Xia said. "And . . . I'm sorry about all that in there, Mr. Gold."

"You have nothing to be sorry for. Not your fault at all."

Everyone entered into Davis's SUV. As they drove away, Jack thought it was good that they had left; they were sending a clear message that the hospitality was lacking. In fact, the Chinese had bungled the entire visit and in the process, demonstrated their disdain for America and its citizens. Never mind that, the Chinese prided themselves on their martial arts proficiency, and Ren had been defeated quickly and brutally, and this after Jack had pleaded with him to stop. Now, they would not just have to support the trade agreement but also earnestly implement it, which would be the best result for *both* countries.

The SUV was suddenly filled with the sound of buzzing; Jack pulled his phone out as the others in the backseat did the same. It was a group text: *Rooms booked at Waldorf Astoria for the four of you. Our sincerest apologies. See you tomorrow at 10am.*

"The Waldorf," Jack said to Davis, slipping his phone back into his pocket.

After they arrived at the hotel and Jack was in his suite, he texted Jojo, sending her the video and a quick message: *It's been a tough day at the office. I'm at the Waldorf. Can you join me? I miss you.*

He put the phone on the bedside table and lay back on the bed. The whole situation was surreal, but he was glad that it hadn't gotten worse—because it certainly could have. He closed his eyes, telling himself he'd rest his eyes until Jojo responded back to him and let him know if she'd be able to make it over or not.

*   *   *

A rhythmic pounding had infiltrated his dream, but as Jack opened his eyes, he realized someone was knocking on the door. He stood up, shaking his head, trying to clear the grogginess.

"Jack?" It was Jojo.

He opened the door. "Hey," he said. She threw her arms around him.

"Are you all right? I texted you back but you never responded."

"Yes, sorry. I fell asleep. Totally didn't mean to. Come on in."

"I'm so sorry about all of that, Jack," she said. "I never knew Ren Yao had that sort of anger inside of him." She gave Jack another hug. "Has my dad seen the video?"

"I sent it to everyone—your dad, Sutton, the press. So if he hasn't yet, he will soon."

"I'm so glad you weren't hurt. Ren Yao definitely won't be going around acting like that anymore. You did the right thing. I'm proud of you and also, embarrassed for my country." She frowned. "It's kind of a weird mix of emotions to be experiencing."

"Do you think your dad will have it censored?"

"I don't know. It doesn't really matter though; this is too big for word not to get out. You were assaulted on a military base by a famous Chinese businessman. He'll pay for that. But seriously, Jack—does the concept of keeping a low profile mean anything to you? You know, keeping more to yourself?"

The truth Jack knew was that a good many Chinese felt as Ren Yao did about America and Americans. While Ren's actions at the hangar were appalling, it would seem Jojo felt the more appropriate response would have been to do nothing. If an American citizen had come in and assaulted a Chinese diplomat during high-level trade talks like Ren did, there was no doubt in Jack's mind many people would have stepped in immediately to stop the altercation.

"I'm a loud, obnoxious American. But you're right. We need to take some time off. We should take Ari up on his offer to visit Israel. Things will probably be a little crazy for a while around here, so if we can skip town for some of that, I think that'd be good. I'll get in touch with Ari and see what his schedule's looking like. And Joshua." Jack paused. "And then have Cooper help arrange things. Would tomorrow be too soon for you?"

"Not at all," Jojo said. "It sounds like letting things cool down here a little bit isn't a bad idea at all."

He sent a message first to Ari, then Joshua, attaching the video to each. Ari replied almost immediately: *You really know how to capture the essence of the moment, Jack. I can fly into Israel tomorrow. Hopefully you won't beat anyone else up between now and then ;)*

Joshua's reply came in a moment later: *Great timing. Lovely video. I've informed the president; see you soon.*

"Okay," he said. "We're all set. Ari and Joshua are going to fly to Israel to meet us there. Let me just send Cooper a text and let him know."

"I'm excited."

Once Cooper had been texted, Jack threw his phone down. "Now that that's taken care of, is there anything else you'd like?"

"I'd like you to pour me a glass of wine and then devour me."

Jack gave her a devilish grin. "Now that's a job I'm up for."

*   *   *

The next morning at ten o'clock, Jack was in one of the conference rooms at the hotel. They would not be returning to Jade Spring Mountain, and would instead hold the second meeting here.

The mood was a bit more somber as people started to file in. Jiang went right over to where Jack was sitting, an apologetic look on his face.

"Good morning," Jack said.

"Good morning, Mr. Gold. I spoke with President Wang last night. Words cannot adequately express how he and the nation feel. He did not censor the video. He thought that would be wrong and that the Chinese people needed to know the truth."

Jack nodded, pleased. "That's certainly refreshing to hear. Thank you. Well, it looks like everyone is here, so why don't we get started. One of the items we need to discuss is Chinese espionage against business-people and academics. And the stealing of military technology. What does everyone think? What should we do?"

Xia raised her hand. "Every country does it. It's not really a trade issue. I think we should skip over it."

Jack looked around. "Does anyone object to skipping over it?"

No one said anything, so Jack continued. "The second issue I have on my list is the shipping of fentanyl from China to America." Jack looked at the Chinese side. "If America was selling opium to China like the Brits did, you'd be up in arms. So I propose that we outlaw the trading, selling, and/or transport of dangerous chemicals, substances, and other materials unless a license is granted. Things like fentanyl, nuclear material. Failure to obtain a license would result in a fine. How much should the fine be?"

"One hundred million?" Tom said.

"No." Jennifer shook her head. "Fentanyl is too profitable. It should be one billion."

"Can we all agree to that?" Jack asked. Everyone nodded. "Okay. I'd now like to move on to three other issues. Now that we will have funds, I'd like to vote that each delegate be paid two hundred thousand dollars per year; attorneys will receive the same, in addition to any other compensation they might be receiving. The translators—who have done a marvelous job—will get one hundred thousand. Agreed?" He watched as everyone raised their hands, looking pleased.

"Great. Second, I think we need to clarify that the president can replace any delegate, at any time, for any reason. I can be replaced with the agreement of both presidents. And third," Jack continued, once everyone had agreed to his second proposal, "I think we need to place in the agreement acknowledgement that a primary goal is to make this organization redundant. The goal is for us not to exist. We need to set milestones for the countries to meet, at which time the moneys they have placed will be returned." He paused, thinking. "Maybe they leave in a nominal amount."

They spent some time discussing the milestones, and once they had an agreeable framework, Jack got up and stuck his head out of the conference room, motioning for Davis, who was standing a few feet down the hallway.

"We're all set in here," Jack said. "We just need to sign the agreement and take some pictures. You feel up for the task?"

"Pictures? Sure thing."

Davis followed Jack into the room. The attorneys were printing the document and then it would be circulated for signing. "I'll be handing you the signed agreement for safe-keeping," Jack said.

He was last to sign the document, and then handed it over to Eric and asked him to scan it and send it to the WeChat group. "Now," he said, passing his phone to Davis. "Let's get a few pictures taken."

The Americans stood and went to stand behind the Chinese delegates, who were still seated. Jack frowned. "No," he said. "That doesn't look right. We shouldn't be standing over you. We should all be sitting or all standing. How about we each stand next to our Monopoly partner, and I'll sit down and hold up the agreement."

Eric gave him the original back and Jack took a seat, the American and Chinese delegates standing with their partners on either side of him.

"Okay," Davis said, holding the phone up. "That looks good. Ready?"

He snapped several photos, and then the attorneys and translators also joined, everyone scrunched together to fit into the photo.

When that was done, Jack went through his phone and sent the photos to the WeChat group. Then he took out his black phone.

> *Please confirm you have the agreement and forward to presidents and public. Pick the photo with the Chinese smiling.*

He slipped the two phones into his pocket and rejoined the group, everyone congratulating each other and shaking hands. It was an historic agreement, and it had gone relatively smoothly, all things considered.

And now that this was completed, it was time to switch gears and get ready to leave for Israel.

CHAPTER 16

In Tel Aviv, Jack and Jojo stayed at the Hoffa Hotel. The gathering at the prime minister's house was not to take place until that evening, so during the day, they met up with Ari and Joshua, who took them on a train ride to Jerusalem, where they explored the Old City and soaked in all the history. They returned to their hotel and relaxed for a few hours before being picked up again to head over to the prime minister's private estate.

The SUV pulled up into a large circular cobblestone drive, but there was no building in sight.

"Where's the house?" Jojo asked. "Don't driveways usually end at a house?"

"Not sure," Jack murmured as they exited.

"This way," Ari said as he circled the front of the SUV. They followed him to a stairway Jack hadn't seen from the car. Down they went, and as they descended, Jack saw a large open-air area set up with twenty large tables in a grove of fig trees. There was a stage in the center, and people were milling about, some had taken their seats already. To his right was an impressive estate with a distinctive Renaissance feel, with its arches and columns.

No sooner had Jack stepped onto the grass at the bottom of the stairs than the prime minister walked over to them and introduced himself.

"Pleasure to meet you," Jack said, shaking his hand. "And this is my fiancée, Jojo."

"Yes, I've heard of you, Jojo, an honor to meet you. Welcome to Israel." He looked at Jack. "Jack? May I borrow you for a moment?"

Before waiting for Jack's reply, he guided him over to the stage and tapped the microphone. "Ladies and gentlemen, please turn off your phones and direct your attention this way." He paused while there was some shuffling. The rest of the people took their seats, and Jack had the growing suspicion that he'd somehow been ambushed. He looked at Jojo, who was with Ari and Joshua at a table near the stage. She had a smile on her face, and when he caught her eye, she winked.

He wasn't accustomed to all this attention. Some people might've reveled in it, but Jack felt it was a bit over the top. He still, after all this, just felt like himself—a regular guy who had found himself in some rather unconventional situations. The prime minister began to speak again.

"I'd like to introduce you all to our guest of honor tonight, Mr. Jack Gold." Everyone clapped politely. Jack smiled as the sides of his face grew hot. "Jack participated in an Israeli military operation. According to all accounts, he deftly entered a Chinese facility and navigated to the objective area. He was then able to enter an ultra-secure facility. But—that isn't all. When a member of the team was incapacitated, Jack, without hesitation, took on that man's duties. And what a duty it was! He had to speak to 1.4 *billion* people—the entire nation of China! He spoke with honesty, intelligence, eloquence, and care." The prime minister paused, letting his words sink in. Jack stood there, unsure of what to do with his hands. He finally settled for interlacing his fingers in front of him. "These are the qualities embodied within Israel," the prime minister continued. He turned to Jack. "You are Jewish, and you are now a citizen of Israel." He reached inside his jacket pocket and pulled out a passport, which he handed to Jack. "Given my authority, I hereby assign you to the Israel Defense Forces."

Where is he going with this? Jack wondered. "Given that you are now a member of the IDF, like your comrades on the mission, I hereby grant to you the Medal of Valor." The prime minister went and stood in front of Jack, affixing the medal on his lapel. "Because of your efforts, China stopped buying oil from Iran, depleting funds that could be used for terrorism. Thank you, Jack, for your service to your country, to your home."

There was hearty applause as the prime minister turned, put his arm around Jack, and smiled for the photographer that had suddenly appeared in front of them. Jack smiled though everything felt surreal— he was now an Israeli citizen? The prime minister had just awarded him the Medal of Valor?

He still felt a little stunned as he went and took his seat next to Jojo, who gave his hand a squeeze.

"Congratulations," she whispered.

The prime minister was still on the stage, and he went back over to the microphone. "Miss Wang, would you join me up here, please?"

Jojo looked at Jack in confusion, but he gave her an encouraging nod and she reluctantly stood up and went and stood where Jack had just been standing.

"You're engaged to Jack, a Jew who has served this country with distinction. Moreover, you are a bright woman who speaks three languages—English, French, and Chinese. You are a talented sculptor and artist. Given my authority, I hereby grant you Israeli citizenship." Again, he opened his jacket and pulled out a passport.

"Me?" Jojo said. "But . . . but I didn't do anything!"

"I spoke with President Sutton, who had talked with President Yang. It is now official; you can legally hold all three passports. Israel and its people welcome you. You are home. Welcome home." He gave Jojo a brief hug and then turned back to the microphone. "And now it's time for festivities! This is an engagement party!"

Jojo came back to the table, holding the passport, a shocked expression on her face. Unlike America and Israel, China would never grant citizenship to a foreigner. "Did that just happen?" she asked. She looked at her passport, then Jack's. "We're Israeli citizens now?"

"And you have the Medal of Valor," Ari said, clapping Jack on the back. "We knew you'd refuse if you knew beforehand, so apologies if this seemed a little like a set-up. Come on, let's mingle—there's lots of people who want to meet you."

For the next hour, Jack made his way around to each table, shaking hands, taking pictures, and being welcomed to Israel. When they returned to the table, Mary had arrived, and Jojo made a beeline for her, the two hugging.

"Let's have some wine," Ari said. He poured a glass for Jack, then Jojo. "This one is from a famous kibbutz known for their great wine. The production is small, though, so none gets exported."

Jack lifted the glass and inhaled, then took a sip. It was smooth, light-bodied but full-flavored.

"Wow," he said, taking another sip. "I think this truly is the best wine I've ever tasted."

"Let's get some food to go with that," Joshua said. "The buffet's over here."

Set out on two long tables were platters of roasted vegetables, lamb and beef kebabs, many types of fruit, humus, pita, salad, olives, and cheese. Everything looked exquisite, and both Jack and Jojo loaded up their plates before returning to the table.

"We have some special entertainment," Ari said. He grinned and raised his eyebrows, though he didn't elaborate, leaving Jack to wonder just what else they had in store for him tonight.

He was almost finished with his food when a little person stepped onto the stage, along with a towering IDF agent. They began to act out a scene, and it took Jack a moment to realize they were role playing what had happened between him and Ren Yao, in a comical variation of David and Goliath.

"That video of you and Ren is all over the place," Ari said. "A bunch of IDF guys have been reenacting the scene and now there's a competition with other security forces to see who can come up with the most outrageous one." Jack looked to the stage, where the little person had just executed the spinning back kick, sending the IDF agent to the ground.

"That one's pretty outrageous," he said, as laughter filled the air around him.

"You haven't seen the one where the transgender woman plays Ren." Ari was laughing so hard he had tears in his eyes.

The next skit featured two women from the IDF. Jack watched as the audience roared their approval. They were acting like it was all a big joke. Something done for their entertainment. He looked at Jojo, who had her hand over her mouth, but that still couldn't conceal her peals of laughter.

They're completely missing the point, he thought.

He considered just gritting his teeth and dealing with it, it would be over soon enough, wouldn't it? But that would be doing exactly what he was upset about in the first place—nothing. And that was the problem with so many people, not just in China, but the whole world over: inaction. Perhaps he had not always taken action when he should have, but lately, he had been doing everything he could. Putting his life in danger for the benefit of a nation, made up of individuals he would never personally meet. His life would have been so much easier if he had never gotten involved with any of this, if he hadn't engaged in the conversation with Ari, if he hadn't gone back into Bar No. 3 to talk to Jojo. Up until this point, though, he would've said that it was worth it, but how could it be worth it when so much of what he had done was now just being viewed as entertainment at a party?

When the skit was over, Jack leaned over to Joshua. "We're going up there for our own reenactment. I want you to announce it to everyone. Tell them to record it if they want. You be Ren." He straightened and looked at Jojo, then Ari and Mary. "You guys seemed to enjoy the show— why don't you join me on stage."

"For what?" Jojo asked.

"You three are going to be the Chinese delegates. Don't worry; all you have to do is sit there. Joshua's going to be Ren."

Ari slapped the table and stood up. "Count me in," he said. He waved his arms in the air. "We have one more skit," he announced to the crowd. "Starring the man who was actually there." There was scattered applause and some rustling as people shifted in their seats.

"Help me grab this table," Jack said to Joshua. There was a small folding table that extra linen napkins and wine glasses had been placed on, and Jack moved those over to the buffet, and he and Joshua carried the table to the stage. They positioned three chairs behind the table and Jack instructed Jojo, Ari, and Mary to take a seat.

"What am I supposed to do?" Jojo whispered.

"You've seen the video," Jack said. "You're one of the Chinese delegates. Do what they did."

Confusion crossed her face. "But . . . they didn't do anything."

Exactly, he thought, but he just gave Jojo a pointed look. "Just be yourself."

"Jack would like to reenact what happened," Joshua said, projecting his voice as he faced the audience. Jojo sat down in between Ari and Mary. "You are all strongly encouraged to video this."

Jack walked back on stage, glad to see that most of the people had their phones out and were recording. Joshua approached him, pushing his head back until Jack fell to the ground. He looked over at Ari, Jojo, and Mary. "Help me," he said. "Stop this."

Jojo glanced at Ari, then back at Jack. "We are not allowed to."

Jack stood up and faced Joshua. "You have just assaulted an American diplomat."

"That was not an assault," Joshua said, without missing a beat. He threw a punch. Jack did exactly as he had done before, except slower, kicking him with his right foot, blocking the blow with his right hand, and then feigning a punch to Joshua's exposed ribs with his left.

He again looked at the Chinese delegates. "Please, do something. Intervene."

But they did nothing. Now, Joshua pretended to kick Jack. Jack grabbed his leg, did a slow back kick to Joshua's groin, but stopped before making any real contact. Jack looked at the delegates again. "I beg you—you must do something."

"We are not authorized," Mary said.

Jack turned and did a slow-motion spinning back kick. Joshua fell to the ground. Jack went over to the microphone. "When an atrocity is occurring, and no one does anything, what does that remind you of?" While what Ren had done to him was nothing compared to the horrors carried out during the Holocaust, the inaction of the bystanders was the same. People witnessed wrongdoing and chose to do nothing.

The audience, who had been laughing, stopped. No one said anything. An uncomfortable silence descended as people exchanged awkward looks with those that sat closest to them.

Jack went and sat down, furious. The only thing people had focused on was what Ren had said and on the actual fight itself. Not one person had seen or understood the significance of the Chinese delegates doing nothing. They, the delegates, were guilty of inaction, an embarrassment to their country because of the system they had grown up within.

But then—someone clapped. It wasn't long before they were joined by someone else, and then it seemed the whole audience was clapping. Jack stood up and gave a brief wave before he sat down. *Thank god Jews are smart*, he thought.

Jojo had a confused look on her face as she came back to the table. He looked at her and felt his anger growing, the words she had spoken to the prime minister not too long ago echoing in his mind.

But I didn't do anything!

"What was that all about?" she asked in a low voice.

"I think we need to call off the engagement," he said.

Her mouth dropped. "Wh . . . what? What do you mean?"

"I don't want to get married to you."

Her eyebrows shot up, then down, and finally, a nervous smile broke out on her face. "You're joking, right? This is a joke. Why would you say that? I must've missed something."

"Yes," Jack said, his tone clipped. "You did miss something. That's a very apt way of putting it."

Relief on Jojo's face. "Okay, phew. Clue me in then, please!"

But he didn't return her smile. It certainly hadn't been his intention, arriving in Israel, to break off his engagement. The realization had dawned on him as he had watched the people reenacting a scene that he had lived out—he, Jack, had done so much for China. He had risked his life on more than one occasion, and not for his personal gain.

"You are no better than the Chinese delegates," Jack said. "You've done nothing. You, of all people, had the power to act, to do something, yet you chose not to. I'm disgusted by that sort of inaction." He stood, ignoring the tears slowly filling Jojo's eyes, the looks of discomfort on Ari and Joshua's face. "Sorry to cut this short," Jack said, "but I'm going to go thank the prime minister again for his hospitality, and then I'll be heading out." He looked at Jojo. "If you want a ride, you can come with me when I'm ready to go, or you can find your own way back."

He realized, as he looked around for the prime minister, amongst the groups of people socializing and drinking, that his abrupt change of mood probably made little sense to Jojo at all. But that shouldn't be surprising—she'd lived her life like so many others had, unwilling to step in, to speak up, to say something. It didn't matter if it was big or small—whether it was addressing a single person or an entire country. Jojo's life was good and she didn't want to do anything to rock that boat. He couldn't tell her what to think or how to behave, but how could he commit to spending the rest of his life with someone like that?

He found the prime minister talking with a small group of people and told him that unfortunately, he had to leave.

"That reenactment of yours—you drive home a very good point," the prime minister said. "A very good point. One that resonates with the people of Israel."

"Well, at least it's resonating with someone," Jack said. He shook the prime minister's hand. "Thank you again for everything."

"Remember, Jack—Israel will always be your home. We would welcome you back any time."

Jack thanked him again. He didn't want to be in Israel right now. He didn't want to go back to China, either.

He could feel Jojo's eyes on him as he walked up the stairs, but she remained in her seat, Ari leaning close and saying something to her. Jack didn't care. He just needed to be somewhere far away from here.

CHAPTER 17

Jack stood at the door of his father's condo in Cabo and took a deep breath. He hadn't been able to stomach the idea of flying back to China, and instead had called his father to see if he could come stay with him for a little while in Montana, thinking Big Sky Country might be the perfect place to clear his head.

"I'm down in Cabo," his father had told him. "You're welcome to come down here if you want. Check out my fly tying skills." He paused. "Everything okay?"

"I'll talk to you when I get there."

So Jack and Davis had flown to Mexico, and Jack raised his arm and knocked on the door. His father answered, wearing blue madras shorts and a short-sleeve, button down shirt. His feet were bare, and he had a deep tan.

"Hey, Dad," Jack said. They hugged, an awkward encounter, as it always had been—neither, it seemed, had ever felt truly comfortable embracing the other.

"How are you, Jack?" his dad asked. "Come on in. I take it those extra guys on the beach are with you?"

"Yeah, sorry about that."

"No need to apologize; I like security. You can never have enough in this day and age, I'm afraid." His father gave him a closer look. "Is that why you're here? Where's Jojo? Actually, don't answer that yet, let's get you in and settled. Want a beer?"

"That'd be great."

"Do you have some shorts in that suitcase?"

"Yeah."

"Why don't you go change then. Guest room is right there down the hall, first room on the right."

Jack went in and changed. He tried not to think about how alone he felt, or what Jojo might be up to. She'd called and sent several WeChat messages, none of which he'd bothered to respond to or even look at. He just wasn't ready yet. And nothing she could say would change his mind, anyway.

He came out of the room in a pair of shorts and a t-shirt. The air was warm and he could smell the ocean air blowing in through the windows. A big sandy expanse of beach and the Pacific Ocean made up his father's backyard.

Jack sat down on the couch across from his father, reaching for the beer on the coffee table. He took a long sip, then another. He sighed.

"So," his father said. "Would you like to tell me why Jojo isn't with you? By the way, that ring you gave her is lovely."

"Well, that's nice that you think so, but we won't be getting married."

If his father was surprised at this news, he didn't show it. "Really. And why is that?"

"We had a falling out. Or I had a falling out. A realization, I guess."

Now his dad gave him a sad, but knowing, look. "Well, you know what I always say." Jack took another swig of beer. Yes, he knew what was next—"If it flies, floats, or fucks—rent it."

He couldn't help but smile, even though he didn't agree. "Great advice, Dad. Really. Stellar. Why has it taken me so long to heed it?"

"You know me, I'm just a treasure trove of good advice. Really, though, Jack, I'm sorry to hear it. Now, I don't know all the details, but maybe . . . maybe you're giving up too easily here. Not everyone can be as perfect as you."

Jack rolled his eyes. "Give me a break. I'm not perfect. And I've never been perfect in your eyes, that's for sure."

His father laughed. "Oh, come on Jack. You know what I'm saying. No one's perfect. I sure as hell am not. And what does it matter what I think, anyway? What matters is what you think. And, if you think that calling off your engagement is the right thing to do, then I trust that you've thought it through. But, sometimes people jump the gun on these sorts of things—usually it's the other way around and they end up in divorce court a few years later—I wouldn't want to see you doing something that you didn't feel right about or weren't ready for. But I talked with your brother not too long ago. He said you and Jojo had a great visit there and that he'd never seen you happier. So . . . I guess I'm just wondering if whatever happened between you and Jojo can be repaired. Did she have an affair?"

"No."

"Did she lie to you in some other way?"

"Not that I'm aware of."

"Did she put another man before you?"

"No." Jack set his beer down and looked out the window. The sun sparkled off the surface of the water. Seagulls squawked. Here he was in paradise, feeling like shit.

"Can we talk about this later?" he asked. "I just need to clear my head. I need to relax."

"Then you've come to the right place. Take as much time as you need. I'm going fishing tomorrow. If you're up for it, let me know."

Jack stretched out on the couch and shut his eyes. "I will," he said. But right now, the only thing he needed to do was take a nap.

*   *   *

Jack spent the next ten days on a true vacation. He didn't sleep late, but instead woke up, went for a jog on the beach as the sun rose, followed by stretching, a series punches, kicks, and karate forms. He wished his morning workout could culminate in a swim, but the currents that came around the Gulf were dangerous, even for the most advanced swimmers. So instead he'd take a shower at the condo, eat breakfast, and relax for the rest of the day.

Sometimes that meant reading, sometimes going for another walk. He went fishing with his father, they went out on his twenty-seven-foot Chris Craft boat, and he chatted with his father's friends who would stop by, of which there seemed to be a never-ending parade.

One evening, Jack made filet mignon with three different types of mushrooms in a cream sauce, topped with fresh parmesan cheese.

"This is delicious," his father said. "I didn't know you could cook so well."

"I enjoy cooking." Jack took a bite. The meat had come out perfectly.

"You're good at anything to which you put your mind." They ate in silence for a few minutes, and then Jack's father put his fork down and looked at him. "I have to ask," he said. "You've been assisting America and China—have they been paying you?"

"No."

"Really. All this work you've done for free?"

"Yes. But I'm still involved with real estate, and I've been fortunate to have had a number of lucrative deals."

His father nodded. "That's good to hear. But most people usually don't work for free. Especially the sort of work that you're doing."

"I guess I didn't really view it as work. It was something I did because it needed to happen for things to evolve in a way that was beneficial for both countries, for citizens of both countries. I wasn't even supposed to be the person speaking to all of China; that was sort of right place at the right time." He reconsidered. "Or maybe wrong place at the wrong time. Whatever it was, I did it because I felt I had to, and because I believe that things can improve for people. But the only way that can happen is if people are willing to act, and don't become complacent and simply expect that someone else is going to take care of it for them." He set his fork down and took a sip of his beer. "And that is, in a nutshell, why Jojo and I are no longer together."

"I'm not following," his father said. "You broke up with her because she didn't do something?"

"That's a very basic way of putting it, but, yes."

"Huh." His father reached for his napkin and dabbed the corner of his mouth, a pensive look on his face.

"What," Jack said. "You disagree with that."

"Well, it's like I said before, Jack. No one's perfect. But you have always excelled at things, and never been afraid to just jump right into the fray. I've read about the Control Center, I've seen pictures of the people you killed. *My god,* I thought when I read that article. *My son has killed people.* Now, they would've killed you if you hadn't beaten them to it, so I'm sure as hell glad you did, but, come on, Jack. This has to stop. You have to untangle yourself from this madness."

"I know."

"And breaking up with Jojo because she might not be as gung-ho as you are about getting right in the thick of things is a little short-sighted, if you want my opinion. That might be the best thing for you. You don't always need to be getting in these dangerous situations. Because some day, it might not work out in your favor."

Jack pushed the rest of his food around on his plate. His appetite was gone.

That evening, he received a text from Andrew, and Jack read it, the first message he'd read and bothered to respond to since he'd arrived.

Long time no see, it read. *When will you be in Shanghai? Stanley and I would like to take you out. Maybe Roosevelt Club again?*

The glow of the phone illuminated his face as he typed a reply. He needed to go back to China, and maybe he'd just plan on moving back to Shanghai. He made plans with Andrew to meet him at the Roosevelt Club at seven that Saturday.

* * *

Jack's father offered to give him a ride to the airport, but Davis was waiting with an SUV to take him.

"You can walk me out, though," Jack said.

Davis got out of the vehicle when they came out, and Jack introduced the two men. "Your son has done some remarkable things for the country," he said. "It's an honor to meet you."

Jack's father smiled. "He has. I'm hoping he'll consider cutting back a little. Just help him stay out of trouble."

"I will, sir."

Davis put Jack's luggage into the back. Jack turned to face his father. "Thanks for letting me crash at your place," he said. He held out his hand, opting for a handshake instead of a hug, a gesture he knew his father would probably appreciate.

"Anytime. Don't go getting involved in anything I wouldn't approve of." He squeezed Jack's hand, didn't let go for a moment. "I'm always here for you."

"I know, Dad. Thank you."

Jack entered into the SUV and put the window down so he could wave goodbye.

Time to go back to China.

CHAPTER 18

He flew into Shanghai and booked a room at the Ritz Portman, where he laid low, ordering room service so he didn't have to leave, until Saturday evening rolled around. It felt strange to be back in Shanghai without Jojo. He still hadn't responded to any of her messages, though he had read some of them. They ran the gamut of confusion, anguish, frustration, sadness.

Jack, why won't you at least explain to me in person what I did that offended you so much?

I'm back in Beijing. Mini misses you. I miss you.

Would you at least respond and let me know you're ok?

I love you. I want to try to work this out.

Jack??

Her last message had been several days ago, and he wasn't sure how he felt about it. Glad that she had given up, that she knew he was serious? Disappointed that she wasn't going to continue to message him every day until she finally heard back?

He showered and changed into a suit and tie and then called a Didi.

"To the Roosevelt Building?" the driver asked when Jack got in.

"Yes."

The driver, a middle-aged man, put his window down and spit. Jack shook his head as the car took off. Yes, definitely back in China.

When he arrived at the Roosevelt Building, he walked in and took the elevator up to the third floor. Andrew was waiting there for him in the lobby.

"Big brother, how are you?" he said. They half embraced, half shook hands, Andrew clapping Jack solidly on the back.

"Glad to be back in Shanghai," Jack said. "Thanks for inviting me out tonight."

"You know I can always find time for you. Come on, let's get you a drink. And a cigar! You deserve it."

Jack followed Andrew down to the cigar room. He greeted Stanley as Andrew went and poured the three of them whiskeys.

"Drink up," he said, handing Jack a very full glass.

"I'm going to be three sheets to the wind if I drink all of this," Jack said. "Jesus, man. You've given me enough for five people."

"Sorry, sorry. I'm just so excited to see you!" Jack raised his eyebrows. He knew Andrew was fond of him, but he seemed exuberant that he was here, and holding a nearly overflowing glass of whiskey.

"We'll be joined by a few others shortly," Stanley said quickly.

"So, what were you doing down in Mexico?" Andrew asked.

Jack sat down on one of the sofas and took a sip of the whiskey. It was good, but there was no way he was going to drink this whole glass. Both Andrew and Stanley had maybe a shot and a half each in their own glasses.

"Here's a cigar."

Jack took the cigar, kept his face impassive as he watched Andrew's eyes dart over to Stanley. Stanley sipped his whiskey, or at least kept bringing the glass up to his lips despite the level of liquid never seeming to decrease.

"So, what were you doing down in Mexico?" Andrew asked again.

"Visiting my dad. I needed to take some time away, clear my head."

"I can only imagine," Stanley said. "You've been quite busy."

"How's your drink?" Andrew asked. "Can I get you some more?"

"Andrew," Stanley said. "Let's not rush the man; let him enjoy his drink in peace."

There was a painting on the wall, above the chair where Stanley sat. Jack nodded to it. "What's that painting?" he asked. "I don't recall seeing it last time I was here."

As Andrew and Stanley swiveled their heads to look, Jack tipped his glass over his shoulder, dumping most of the whiskey onto the carpet behind him. He brought the glass up to his lips right as they turned back, draining the last drops.

"Oh that?" Stanley said. "It's nothing special, just a colonial painting of a traditionally dressed woman." He raised his eyebrows, seeing Jack's empty glass. "Well, Mr. Gold, you can certainly hold your liquor."

Andrew immediately hopped up and retrieved the whiskey bottle, poured more for Jack.

"No need for such a heavy pour this time," Jack said. "A little will do. Thank you, gentlemen. I needed this."

Andrew set the bottle down and held up his glass. "To friends!"

Jack raised his own glass and downed its contents. Andrew and Stanley seemed to be looking at him more closely now, as if trying to gauge just how intoxicated he was.

What is going on, Jack thought. Something was up.

"If you two will excuse me for a moment," Stanley said. "I have to make a brief phone call, but I'll be right back."

He exited the room. Jack pulled his phone out, making like he was checking the time. Instead, he turned his voice memo on record before slipping it back into his pocket. He looked at Andrew. "So," he said. "How have you been? I feel like all these questions so far have been directed at me."

Andrew tapped his right foot incessantly. He was either very anxious about something or had downed a bunch of espresso right before Jack arrived. "I have a problem," he said. "And that problem is that I can't find any good marijuana. I bet you could've brought me some good stuff from California. Or Mexico! You should do that for me."

Jack smiled. "That's not the worst problem in the world to have. How's business?"

"It's booming. I'm off the Wuxi project and we've signed two others. Thanks to you and the trade agreement, the building cycle is really ramping up. We're in the right place at exactly the right time."

The door opened and Stanley came back in the room, an apologetic smile on his face. "Sorry about that," he said. "Who's up for one more drink? To the trade agreement."

Jack stood up and retrieved one of the unopened water bottles that was sitting at the center of the table. "To the trade agreement."

"Jack," Andrew said. "You can't toast with water."

"He's right," Stanley said. "The trade agreement is such a significant accomplishment. Let Andrew pour you one more drink."

"To you and Andrew, and the trade agreement." Jack twisted the cap off and took a sip of the water. No sooner had he replaced the cap when the door opened again.

Mr. Big walked in, followed by another man Jack had never seen before. The man locked the door and then stood there, arms crossed.

They set me up, Jack thought, dropping the water bottle. He didn't even bother to look at Andrew or Stanley, instead focusing all his attention on Mr. Big. He walked toward him. "It's nice to see you again."

As Jack approached, Mr. Big backed up, trying to increase the distance between the two of them. "I've been waiting for this day since we last met," he said, a smile on his round face. "My colleagues were unsuccessful in Arizona, but I have a good friend to introduce you to. His name is Xin Xin."

Xin Xin uncrossed his arms and took a step forward. He was older than Mr. Big, and taller, with a slim physique that Jack knew he should not underestimate. He smiled, and as he did so, Jack saw two rows of perfectly straight white teeth. Xin Xin reached inside his blazer's jacket and pulled out two ten-inch blades. The blades gleamed in the light and looked like they had been freshly sharpened. *Xin*, Jack knew, meant "heart" in Chinese, and there was no doubt in his mind this man standing in front of him could most certainly cut out two hearts at once.

Well, great. Jack took a deep breath, felt like the air was tingling around him. He was way out of his league here, but he sure as hell wasn't about to let them know it. Jack moved his arms down at his side. There was little they could do against such sharp knives. Xin Xin was a professional, someone who had probably killed dozens, if not hundreds. Jack's karate skills might buy him a little time, but he was no match for a person of this caliber.

He had a feeling everyone in the room knew it, too.

Time seemed to freeze. Xin Xin stood in front of him, knives brandished. Jack's life didn't flash before his eyes, rather, it was the possibility of just admitting defeat and succumbing to whatever end Xin Xin had in mind. There'd be some pain, but then it would be over and . . . rest? That didn't sound so bad. It wasn't like he had that much to look forward to, anyway. All the financial success in the world meant nothing if his personal life was in shambles.

"Let's have a seat and enjoy the show," Mr. Big said. "Pour me some of that whiskey. As promised, I'll be rewarding the two of you handsomely."

His words snapped Jack back to reality. No, this was not how it ended for him, not at the hands of some contract killer, set up by someone he considered both a colleague and a friend. Xin Xin advanced, moving both the blades in a rhythmic circle in front of him. Jack took a few steps back, trying to give himself a moment to figure out a strategy.

The knives were long enough that they could cut his arms if he tried to punch. Jack considered a back kick but knew he'd be stabbed in the back as he turned around. Xin Xin lunged forward, aiming a blade at Jack's stomach. Jack hopped back, curving in his stomach so the blade could not reach him. Jack looked down at Xin Xin's wrist—too far away to grab. Xin Xin was just warming up, toying with him. Jack had to do something. He kicked out low with his right foot, taking aim at Xin Xin's left ankle. One of the blades nicked his shin and Jack felt the warm trickle of blood, but the blade was so sharp the cut hadn't hurt at all. He kicked out again, this time using the other leg, receiving another superficial cut as he did so.

Xin Xin lunged at him and Jack jerked to the side, just missing what could have easily been a devastating slash. He kicked out again with his right foot then left foot, watching as Xin Xin bent slightly to try to cut his leg. Then, on his next low kick, at the last instant he kicked upward, making direct contact with Xin Xin's jaw, his head snapping back violently.

Before he was able to orient himself, Jack launched himself directly into Xin Xin, knocking him down. He landed squarely on his chest, making sure to grab both of the man's wrists to neutralize the knives. He twisted his wrists back, trying to force him to drop the blades, but Xin Xin was strong and seemed impervious to the pain Jack was trying to inflict. He pushed back against Jack, and though the man was older and slimmer than he was, Jack could feel he would overpower him in a few seconds. He let go of Xin Xin's wrists and jammed his thumbs into the man's eye sockets. Xin Xin flailed, the knives slicing Jack's arms, legs. But he didn't relent, leaning as much of his body weight as he could into his arms, his thumbs. Blood and tears pooled and then began dribbling out the sides of Xin Xin's eyes. He continued to apply pressure until he felt Xin Xin's eyeballs collapse underneath the weight, like little stress balls that had been squeezed too tightly.

He pulled his arms back, wiped his hands on the rug. Xin Xin was still alive but barely, and wouldn't be getting up any time soon. Jack snatched the knives away and used one to inflict a deep slash across Xin Xin's throat. Blood poured out and his body stilled.

Jack stood, both knives now in his possession. His arms and legs had been cut, but he'd taken no significant damage. He faced the three men, all standing, mouths agape.

"Here you go," Jack said, holding one of the knives out to Mr. Big. "The final encore. Let's go."

Mr. Big took the knife and examined it. Then he lunged.

Jack took a step back and Mr. Big missed him completely. He turned to try to strike again, but this time, Jack shifted to the side, stepping forward simultaneously, as he jammed his own blade right in the soft area where the chin curves down to the throat. Jack thrust upward, all the way into the brain. He gave the knife a little twist as Mr. Big's eyes widened, and then it was lights out. Jack let go of the knife as Mr. Big slumped to the floor.

He turned. Stanley and Andrew hadn't moved, sheer terror on their faces at the sight of so much blood. Andrew was white as a sheet.

"I think I'm going to—"

He didn't have a chance to finish; he turned and vomited onto the carpet.

Jack reached for his phone to photograph what happened, but felt a sudden vertigo slam into him, knocking everything sideways. Was he still standing? He was trying to get his bearings when darkness suddenly engulfed him.

CHAPTER 19

Jack wasn't sure how long he'd been asleep for when he finally managed to pry an eyelid back, then his other, to find himself staring at a ceiling he didn't recognize.

Voices, to his right—Jojo and her father.

He turned his head slowly, saw the two of them sitting there, heads close together, not looking at him as they spoke in hushed tones. Just the sight of Jojo brought tears to his eyes and he turned back, not wanting her to see. He let his eyes close as he listened to them speak in Suzhou dialect. Jojo's tone was forceful, and from the sounds of it, she was admonishing her father.

He kept his eyes closed as he lay there, half-dozing. The conversation had stopped, and he wondered if he was in the room alone. No sooner did he think that, though, when he felt Jojo take his hand, entwine her fingers with his own. "Get better, Jack. Please. I'm so sorry about everything."

Jack managed to pry his eyelids up again. Jojo was a blur until he blinked several times, and slowly she came into focus, her dark hair flowing down over her shoulders, her eyes focused on him, worry etched across her face.

"Hey," he said, voice scratchy like he was getting over a bout of laryngitis. He coughed. His whole body felt strange and he could tell that someone must've given him something because everything in his head felt slow and syrupy. But one thing he was certain he felt was overwhelming relief to see Jojo there by his bedside.

"Jack," she said, her fingers tightening around his, a smile coming to her face. "How are you feeling?"

"Okay, I think," he said. "I feel a little funny, but . . . not too bad." An image of Xin Xin on the ground, bleeding from his eye sockets, Mr. Big with the knife jammed through his skull, flashed through Jack's mind and he tried to push it away, focus on Jojo. Things could have ended much differently, yet for whatever reason, they had not. What had he been so upset with Jojo over anyway? It was hard to recall. He felt as if he had been given a second chance, and this realization once again brought tears to his eyes.

"Oh, don't cry," Jojo said. "You're going to be just fine. The American Embassy is overseeing your care, and you're in good hands. They had to give you a blood transfusion and some stitches, but it's nothing that you won't recover from fully." She reached down and gently wiped away one of the tears that had slipped down his cheek.

"I'm so glad you're here." It would have been so awful to wake up and be alone, or wake up to a nurse or doctor's unfamiliar face. "I love you, Jojo."

Her eyes widened. "I love you, too, and I've wanted to talk to you so badly after what happened in Israel, but you wouldn't—"

"None of that matters," Jack said.

"What are you talking about? Of course it matters. You were totally right. That was what I was talking to my dad about a little while ago. Do you know what I told him? That I was embarrassed to be Chinese. That I was embarrassed to be his daughter, as the president of this nation, if we were just going to sit by and do nothing. I told him to open the country up. I received more love and stimulation in the short time I was in Israel and America than I've ever gotten in my home country. Everyone in China is the same. There is no diversity. How messed up is that?"

Jack smiled. "You really said all that to your dad?"

"I did, and more. I admit, Jack, I was hurt and upset by what you said. But then I had time to think about it, and I realized that everything you said was right. You, one individual person, has done so much for China. And you're not even from China! I told my dad, if he didn't open the country, I was going to leave forever and never speak to him again."

"You wouldn't have to do that."

"I meant it. No more just sitting around and doing nothing."

"Oh, I believe you."

"But if I was going to leave, I'd want it to be with you." Now it was Jojo's eyes filling with tears. "It's been so awful these past few weeks, not being able to see you, not even being able to talk to you. I've missed you so much."

An American doctor came in, and Jojo quickly wiped at her eyes. "How are you feeling, Mr. Gold?" he asked. He was young, maybe a few years younger than Jack.

"Not so bad, all things considered," Jack said. "I'm a little thirsty."

"I'll get you some water." The doctor came over with a large plastic cup with a lid and a flexible straw. Jojo helped Jack sit up. So long as he went slowly, nothing hurt too badly. He let Jojo hold the cup while he took a sip, then another, the cool water soothing his throat.

"How long do I have to stay here?" Jack asked. "I'd like to get home as soon as possible."

The doctor looked down at the tablet he was carrying, tapped a couple times on the screen. "You'll need to stay at least two nights so we can keep an eye on your stitches. Did they tell you how many you had?"

"No."

"Fifty-five." The doctor raised his eyebrows. "That's a rather significant number of stitches. And we don't want to see any infection set in, so we'd like you to stay here at least the two nights, and then we'll see how you're feeling and how the stitches are looking. The best thing you can do right now is just rest."

"Fair enough," Jack said. "I don't feel like I'd be up for much else now anyway. Hey, I do have one question though." He looked at Jojo with a smile. "Can she spend the night?"

"Yes. No sex, though." He blanched a little. "Not to be presumptive . . ."

Jojo laughed. "We'll behave."

After the doctor left, Jojo helped Jack arrange the pillows behind him so he could sit up. He felt more awake now, the sedative must've been wearing off, and with his alertness, he also became aware of the discomfort in his extremities. He looked at his forearms and saw the sewn-up lacerations, the way his skin was stretched tight and slightly swollen.

"Held together by some thread," he said. "These are going to itch like crazy in a day or two, I can tell."

There was a knock at the door and Davis appeared, looking about ten years older than the last time Jack saw him.

"Jack!" he said. "I didn't think you'd be awake and sitting up. But I'm glad to see it." He looked at Jojo. "I hope I'm not interrupting anything."

"No, no," Jojo said. "Come on in. The doctor just came by and told us that Jack had to spend the next two nights, but if things look good after that, he can go home."

Davis nodded. "Glad to hear it."

"What the hell happened, Davis?" Jack asked.

Davis sat down in one of the chairs next to the bed. Jack could see the deep lines etched on his face. "They jammed our equipment, but we held off entering, thinking they hadn't even arrived. They came in through a basement entrance unknown to the Chinese. If we had people stationed outside your door, it wouldn't have happened. We all took a risk and are just glad you're okay."

"Was there audio from my phone?"

"Yes. Your phone kept recording when the signal jamming occurred. We sent that, along with photos, to DC. A press release was put out by both the U.S. and China. There were no pictures included."

"Too graphic?"

"Yes. The pictures were gruesome. You gouged one guy's eyes out and put a knife through the other's brain. The guys at Langley saw the two knives and wondered how the hell you were able to make it out of there alive."

"I wonder that myself, to be honest." Jack paused. "What about Andrew and Stanley?"

"The audio clearly implicates them. They've both been arrested. With the evidence we gave to China, justice will be fair and swift."

It was the best outcome he could hope for; he didn't want to let himself sink too deep in the mire of Andrew's betrayal, but Jack did feel stung by it.

"Okay," Jack said finally. "Good to know. I guess I'll just be resting here for the next couple of days."

"You do that." Davis stood up. "I'd pat your shoulder but I don't know where they've sewn you up and where they haven't, so . . . rest up, Jack."

"I will."

After Davis left, Jack stifled a yawn. He hadn't been awake for that long, but he already felt drowsy and ready to go back to sleep.

Jojo moved two of the pillows so he was able to lie back. "Will you come lie with me?" he asked.

"Of course."

"And before I drift off to sleep, would you arrange for us to visit your dad, say, in five days or so?"

"Sure. Will you be up for that?"

"Yes. Tell him I'd like to drink some Maoti with him and sign our marriage documents. He can arrange for someone from Suzhou to come to Beijing to process things, I'm sure."

Jojo held her left hand up, looking down at the red diamond. Tears came to her eyes. "Nothing would make me happier."

CHAPTER 20

Jack looked at himself in the bathroom mirror. He was freshly showered and had on a traditional Chinese black silk shirt and khaki pants. He'd stayed the two days at the hospital, as required, and then had been allowed to return home, where he'd enjoyed the past four days being looked after by both Jojo and the dog, who didn't seem to want to leave his side.

He left the bathroom, glad that he'd be getting most, if not all, of his stitches out the following week. The itching had set in and sometimes it was so intense he felt like he was about to jump out of his own skin. Jojo would pat the area, which alleviated the itch a little bit.

"Beautiful," Jack said, when he saw Jojo. She was wearing makeup and had on a perfect-fitting yellow Cheongsam dress, her hair swept up in a bun, accentuating her beautiful features. "You look incredible."

She smiled when she saw him. "So do you. And don't forget your passport!"

Jack patted his pocket. "I have it."

They bid goodbye to Mini and the two of them stepped outside, where a Hongqi limousine was waiting. The long, sleek black car, with its shiny white rims was the epitome of elegance and the perfect vehicle to take them to Zhongnanhai to get their marriage certified.

The roads had been cleared, and onlookers stood on the side to watch as the lone car drove by.

"I guess this is how celebrities must feel," Jack said, looking out at the faces that couldn't see him because of the tinted windows. "I still just feel like a regular guy though."

"That's a good thing," Jojo said.

They entered Zhongnanhai and saw beautiful flowers everywhere— yellow orchids, red and pink roses, gladiolus. When they exited, Jack took a deep breath and could smell lavender in the air.

"This is more than the simple administrative session I thought it was going to be," Jack whispered to Jojo as she stepped out of the car. Her eyes widened.

"Me too," she said, taking his hand.

A man and a woman stood at the entrance, waiting to greet them. They escorted them inside and into an elegant room that reminded Jack of the Red Room in the White House, except this room had purple and yellow orchids placed on the long oval table in front of them.

"Please, have a seat," the woman said. "May I get you some tea?"

"That would be lovely, thank you," Jojo said.

A moment after the woman exited, President Wang entered the room. "Please, don't get up, Jack," he said, when Jack started to rise. Wang went over and took Jack's hand. "I was worried about you. You've made an excellent recovery so far. I cannot express how sorry I am for everything, but I hope I will be able to over time."

"Thank you," Jack said. "But you don't need to apologize."

The woman came back in with a tea tray and poured cups for the three of them.

"Thank you," Jack said. The photographer came into the room and gave Wang a brief nod, then began setting up his tripod.

"Shall we get started?" Wang asked.

"Yes," Jojo said. She gave Jack's hand a squeeze.

Wang gave the photographer a brief nod, and the man began directing Jack and Jojo, having them stand next to each other in front of the red wall. It was easy to smile for the photos; Jack felt safe and happy here with Jojo and her father.

The photographer took about a dozen photos, and then asked them to choose their favorite.

"I like that one," Jojo said. In the photo she chose, neither were looking directly at the camera; instead, she had a big smile on her face as she looked up at Jack, and he had his head tilted slightly back, clearly in the middle of a laugh. It was the most candid out of all the shots, and Jack felt it best captured who they really were. Jojo picked out a second, more formal photo where they were both looking at the camera for the legal document certifying their marriage.

"Perfect," Jack said.

They went back and finished their tea. A woman with short, dark hair came in, carrying a briefcase. She greeted them before sitting down and taking out the Marriage Registration forms for Jack and Jojo to fill in. Jack struggled given his poor Chinese writing skills.

"Are you freely agreeing to marry?" the woman asked.

"Yes," they said simultaneously.

"May I see your ID and passport, please."

They handed over the documents and the woman looked at Wang. "President Wang, do you have the Household Registry Booklet?"

"Yes," Wang said, taking the dark red booklet from his pocket and handing it over. The Hukou system worked as a family registration program, and the book contained a record of births, deaths, marriages, divorces, and moves within a family.

Jack and Jojo drank more tea as the woman wrote in the booklet. Then, she gave Jack and Jojo their own larger red booklet, which was their marriage certificate.

They looked at each other, smiling. They were married. Jack leaned in and gave Jojo a kiss.

When they pulled apart, everyone stood up. Wang looked at them earnestly. "You must try your best to understand each other throughout your lives. If you have any problems, you should work them out. Living a simple life with the one you love is the most important."

Jack listened to his guidance carefully, knowing this was not a casual moment. After Wang finished Jojo grabbed both of his hands. "Thank you, Dad."

Wang looked directly to Jack. "Oh, and I'm not giving my daughter away to your family; you are joining ours."

Jack shook his father-in-law's hand. "With pleasure."

Wang beamed. "Good. Now it's time for some Maotai."

The woman who had brought them tea came in with a tray holding the bottle of Maotai and three glasses.

"May your marriage be peaceful, passionate, and prosperous," Wang said. Jack winked at Jojo and held up his glass.

"Speaking of prosperous," Wang said after he took a long sip, "I have some good news for you, Jack. But first I'm wondering if you might give me some more details as to how things transpired in the Roosevelt Room, if you don't mind me asking."

Jack glanced at Jojo, who gave a slight nod. "Sure," he said. He took another sip of his drink, and then proceeded to explain to Wang exactly what happened, starting with Andrew's clumsy efforts to get him inebriated.

"I can't believe I married a stone-cold killer," Jojo said with a smile when Jack had finished.

Wang shook his head in amazement. "You're a lucky man, Jack. And now, a much wealthier one, too."

Jack looked at him. "What do you mean?"

"There was a bounty on both Xin Xin and Zhang Zhong. It'll be deposited into your Bank of China account in a few days."

"A bounty?"

"Yes. One hundred million RMB on Xin Xin; much higher on Zhang Zhong, given his crimes. Two hundred and fifty million."

Jack's jaw dropped. That was about 50 million U.S. dollars.

"I spoke with Sutton," Wang continued, "and the money will not be taxed in America or China. Neither country paid you for your assistance in the trade negotiations, so, we think that's fair."

"Yes, quite fair."

Jojo held her glass up. "I think this calls for another toast—to being alive, and to family."

"I can drink to that," Jack said.

"There's one more thing I'd like to mention for your consideration," Wang said. "There are two things that I think should occur. One is that I need to address the nation about a few things. I need to right some wrongs." He looked at Jojo, then Jack. "At the same time, I think it would be nice if you had a wedding celebration. Something fun. Your wedding reception will be of national interest—whether you like it or not, you are both famous. I propose we have what the nation wants: a big televised reception, at least for the first hour. And you two won't have to worry about planning a thing, you just need to show up and enjoy yourselves."

"Where would it be held?" Jojo asked.

"If we do it next month when the weather's nice it could be at the Forbidden City. If the weather isn't cooperating, we can just use the West Wing of the Meridian Gate."

Jojo's eyes widened. "Dad!"

"It's right next-door. One hundred and eighty acres. We'll occupy a small fraction of that space. The leadership are getting old; they can walk there. And like I said, we'd only use part of it, maybe just the Imperial Garden."

Jojo looked at Jack. He smiled. "I don't mind having a reception where twenty-four emperors previously lived," he said. "I have a suggestion, too."

"I'd love to hear it," Wang said.

"Well, everyone is going to be wondering how Jojo and I met. What if Jojo writes it down, and then at the reception, someone can read it. The nation will hear and feel like they are a part of it. We can use our love to help unify the country."

"Brilliant," Wang said. "Jack, you're obviously familiar with message reinforcement. Have you ever considered going into politics?"

Jack smiled. "I find it's far easier to get things done when you're not a politician."

"You're very wise." Wang opened his jacket and took a folded piece of paper out of his pocket, which he handed to them. "This is the deed to your house, and I am giving it to you as a wedding present. The lease is for seventy years, and you'll easily be able to renew it if you decide to do so."

"Oh my gosh," Jack said. "Thank you."

Jojo looked up from the paper. "Dad, that's so generous."

Wang waved them off. "Please. It's the least I could do. We'll have someone visit regularly to take care of anything that might need fixing, and we'll get you some people to help with the landscaping. You can tell them what you want planted and they'll take care of it."

Jack and Jojo looked at each other. "Watermelon," they both said.

Wang grinned. "Let's drink to that!"

CHAPTER 21

Jack watched as President Wang stood on a terrace, overlooking the eight hundred guests for the wedding reception. Wang wore a conservative dark gray suit with a red tie, and in front of him, were two video recording stations broadcasting live through the CCTV Building.

"Hello, ladies and gentlemen," he said. "Thank you for coming tonight to celebrate the marriage of my daughter, Jojo, to Jack Gold." He turned and smiled at them before looking back to the audience. "Before beginning the celebration, though, there are a few things I need to say. I consider myself lucky to be welcoming Jack into my family, as my son-in-law, but, as a nation, we should *all* consider ourselves fortunate for Jack, who many of you saw for the first time when he addressed our country at the Control Center. He also played a vital role in the trade agreements. For his efforts, he's been assaulted and two attempts have been made on his life. He received over fifty stitches. And no one, as far as I know, has thanked him for his contribution. To make matters even worse, no one stood up for or helped him when he was in danger. We owe Jack our gratitude and sincerest apologies from the entire Chinese population. No more can we sit idly by while atrocities occur. Teachers, teach your students. Parents, instruct your children."

Wang paused. He cleared his throat, then coughed. He turned away from the microphone and coughed again, a dry, unproductive sound. He reached for a glass of water. Jack glanced at Jojo as Wang's coughing attack subsided.

"He had that cough a few days ago," Jojo murmured. "It doesn't sound good. He thinks it might be leftover from that time he was really sick a little while ago."

Jack frowned, Jojo's words stirring up thoughts of the neurotoxin Jack had infected Wang and others with. Was it possible it had evolved?

Could Wang have gotten re-infected? Jack swallowed and forced the thought from his mind. He was supposed to enjoy the day, and it was most likely just a cold anyway.

Wang resumed speaking, his cough now under control. "As the new trade agreement gets implemented," Wang said, "China will grow. To really grow, China needs the smartest and the brightest. Therefore, we must be open and welcoming to people outside of our country. Currently, we are not an international country. Foreigners constitute zero percent of the population. Singapore, a tiny country, has twice as many foreigners. We do not need to fear diversity. Rather it is essential for innovation. We need more people from other countries to be accepted in China, not just drained of their knowledge and thrown away." Wang paused. "And, lastly, the Chinese language is a very difficult language. As non-native speakers come from other countries, it will be useful for all Chinese to also speak English, and to start learning from an earlier age. Our teaching system and methods must be improved, and this needs to be a national priority."

Wang glanced over his shoulder at Jack, and when their eyes met, the two exchanged a smile. Wang looked back at the crowd. "But today is about celebrating the marriage of Jojo and Jack. And as part of that, they would like to share their story with all of you, in Jojo's own words."

Wang stepped back from the microphone as a young woman dressed in white approached. She was holding the pages Jojo had written, and she waited until a hushed silence descended before she began to read. "*I'm a sculptor, but sometimes I work odd jobs because I like to get inspiration. I was working at bar when I met Jack . . .*"

And as their story, in Jojo's words, was read to the live audience of eight hundred, and who knew how many more watching at home, Jack sat back and let himself be awash in the memories of his early days with Jojo, which seemed like so long ago, yet, in retrospect, really weren't.

But of course it would seem that way, he reasoned, so much had happened. He smiled as the woman read Jojo's words about the lamb and curry dish he had made on one of their early dates.

"*My stomach told my heart this was my man,*" the woman said, and Jack smiled and gave Jojo's hand a squeeze.

He was surprised to hear, as the woman continued reading, that Jojo detailed their breakup in Israel, placing the blame fully on herself.

"*My life was shattered*," the woman read. "*The man I loved was disgusted with me, because like so many others in this country, I had chosen to do nothing . . .*"

As she continued to read, hope surged through him—hope that things would change for the better. That everything he had done, all the risks he had taken, the attempts on his life, that it wasn't all for no reason.

When the woman finished reading, she turned from the microphone, wiping tears from her eyes. Wang gestured to stand and come greet the crowd.

"Ready?" Jojo asked as they stood up. Jack gave her hand another squeeze.

"Ready," he said.

They walked toward the terrace railing. Wang smiled and took Jojo's hand. With his other hand, he took Jack's, and then he brought their hands together. He let go and stepped back, and Jack and Jojo faced the roar of approval from the crowd. Still holding hands, they raised their arms up, smiling at each other before looking out at the sea of faces. He caught sight of the cameras, broadcasting them to millions of households across China.

This was the start of something new—not just for him and Jojo as newlyweds, but for the country as a whole, Jack was certain of it.

Please leave a review
and if you have any inquiries visit
www.bradleygood.com

THE PROBABILITY OF SUCCESS

THE CHINA AFFAIRS

BOOK 3

CHAPTER 1

Sometimes, Jack Gold found he still marveled at the fact of everyday technology—things that would have sounded like science fiction only a few generations prior—that people all over the world took for granted now, like the fact that so many now walked around with a tiny computer in their pockets, the world's wealth of knowledge just a few finger swipes away.

Jack poured some coffee out of the French press as he waited for his father to answer his FaceTime call. Jojo's dog, Mini, a border collie mix, followed Jack back to the living room and lay at his feet. Jack's father's face suddenly appeared on the laptop screen.

"Jack," his dad said. "Hi. I knew it was you—you're the only who calls me with FaceTime."

"Hi Dad," Jack said. His father, who lived year-round in Cabo after retiring from a successful ob-gyn practice, looked tanned and relaxed. "And you know I call you on FaceTime so I can better tell if you're bull-shitting me or not." Jack's dad smiled. "How is living in Cabo year-round anyway?"

"Can't complain. I can go fishing anytime I want. Weather's always beautiful. After seeing patients for thirty-five years, I think I've earned it."

"No one's going to argue with that," Jack said. Of course his father would feel he had to "earn" any leisure time he now had—he'd ingrained that exact sentiment into Jack from an early age.

"How are you?" his father asked. "How's Jojo?"

As if on cue, Jojo came into the room, smothering a yawn, her hair still a little messed up from sleeping. "Hello, Dr. Gold," she said in English, with a slight French accent, as she pulled a chair closer to Jack. "I'm still not fully awake yet."

Jack's father smiled. "Hi, Jojo. You're looking great, fully awake or not. You've gained a little weight—it suits you."

Leave it to his dad to instantly notice such a little thing from seven thousand miles away. Jack put his arm around his wife's shoulders. "Dad, we do have some news we'd like to share with you. Jojo is three months pregnant. So . . . it would appear you are going to be a grandfather."

"You don't say." The smile that had been on his father's face was replaced with a look of surprise, which quickly morphed into another smile, this one congratulatory in nature, but also, Jack felt, a little forced. "Congratulations to both of you. You'll be excellent parents."

Jojo seemed to take him at his word, but Jack knew his father was less than thrilled about his impending grandfather-hood when he immediately pivoted the conversation to another topic.

"So, Jack, what have you been up to? Did you find a job? Are you making any money?"

The answer to the last two questions was no, which made Jack uncomfortable to admit, despite the fact that he did not need a job. He had risked his life on more than one occasion in his bid to help the citizens of China have more say over their own lives, and he'd been paid handsomely. But for all his previous efforts, he was realizing how difficult sustained human change really was. With the help of his good friend Ari, he had addressed the nation of China, from the country's very own Control Center. The previous administration was removed and Jack's own father-in-law was named the president. Yet despite having more freedom now, the average Chinese citizen did little to exercise those freedoms, and this surprised Jack.

"I'm taking some time to chill out," Jack told his father. "Things will come together, and I've got more than enough money. The bounty for those two guys was about fifty million. We're doing okay right now."

His father raised his eyebrows and nodded. "Yes, I'd say you are. Though a man your age should still find a way to meaningfully contribute, I never understood these people that take an early retirement in their fifties, some of them even in their forties. You've got a lot of useful years left, Jack, don't let them go to waste just because your bank account's flush."

Jack sighed. "I won't, Dad."

"Think you'll have the chance to visit before the birth?"

Jack glanced at Jojo. She gave him a smile and then turned her attention to the laptop screen. "We would certainly like that," she said. "We'll have a better idea on things within the next few weeks; we still haven't seen a doctor so it's a little early to plan long-distance travel."

"We're here all the time so you can come whenever's convenient. Jack, I want to take you marlin fishing, this season should be great. Remember that huge one you caught when you were eight?"

"How could I forget?" Jack asked. That had been one of his life experiences he'd never forget, despite that it had happened decades ago, when Cabo was still just a fishing village and not a thriving tourist destination. His father had been the one to hook the marlin, but he'd handed Jack the fishing rod. "It's yours!" he'd told him.

Finally, he would get to catch a huge marlin like his father had done so many times before. Even now as an adult Jack could recall how that exact excitement felt, rushing through him as he gripped the rod and tried to reel in the fish. But that excitement started to wither as the fish's resistance increased and his hands began to ache. He'd reel the fish in a little only to have it pull the opposite direction a moment later. It was a never-ending cycle, the truest example of *one step forward, two steps back.*

After thirty minutes, his hands were rubbed raw and bleeding. But the fish's resolve was wavering, its strength ebbing. Jack was keenly aware of his father's gaze on him.

"Come on, Jack," his dad said to him. "You got this. Never quit. Reel him in. Keep the rod high so the line doesn't break!"

Even now, years later, the conversations, the feel of his blistered hands, the weight of his father's gaze, his expectations—it was as easy to recall as if it had happened yesterday.

"I'd love to catch another big one," Jack said.

"Well, it's not going to happen unless you come out here."

"We're going to try to make it happen, Dad," Jack said. "Things have really settled down for us, so I'm sure I'll be seeing you sooner rather than later."

"Okay, good. Keep me posted. Jojo, congratulations. I'm excited for you both."

They said their goodbyes and Jack disconnected the call. Jojo stretched and yawned. "You know, I think I'm going to go back to bed for a little while."

Jack took a sip of his coffee. He wanted to follow Jojo back to bed, but he felt mildly unsettled. Was it that he sensed his father was not really that excited about the baby? Or that his father disapproved of the fact he wasn't working, despite the multimillions he had in his bank?

"Get some more rest," Jack said. "I'll try to keep it down out here."

"I'm glad I overheard you and got to say hi to your dad. He seemed excited to hear the news!"

Jack did not dispute this, though he disagreed with Jojo on that point. She squeezed his shoulders. "You're tense."

"I must've been a little nervous to tell my dad the news," he said. "But yeah, he took it pretty well."

Jojo went back into their bedroom. Jack found himself thinking about his dad, both the dad of his childhood and his dad now, retired. The dad of his childhood worked all the time, at the hospital, helping others, saving people's lives. Often, it would be in the middle of the night or at some other inopportune time, like a birthday party or a holiday. His dad now was retired and lived in Cabo where he spent his days fishing, reading, relaxing on the beach. Jack had the financial wherewithal to do the same, but he'd not put his time in, the way his father had. Never mind that he'd gone to a great college, an excellent graduate school, spoke fluent Chinese, and had helped both China and America. Jack had tried—and mostly succeeded—to excel in everything he did. He always finished a job because that was how he'd been programmed. That was the example he'd seen growing up and that was the sentiment that was hardwired into him. Living a life of leisure had to be earned through long hard work, and Jack knew that in his father's eyes, he hadn't earned it yet.

Could his dad ever change? Would he ever stop having such expectations? But really, did the fabric of a man or woman ever really change? It was nearly impossible, Jack knew; he shouldn't expect his father to change any more than he could expect himself to change. He had always tried to accept his father for who he was: a hard worker, someone others could count on, a man who kept his cards close and did not ever see the value in showing his affection, at least to his children. Jack could not ever recall his father giving him a hug or speak of his feelings beyond the superficial small talk people engaged in when first beginning a conversation.

Maybe my dad's actually Chinese, Jack thought, smiling. Showing affection or talking about love were not things most Chinese people felt comfortable doing. Fortunately, Jojo did not fall into this category.

Turning his attention back to the computer screen, Jack saw an advertisement for cruises going to Cabo. His mind drifted for a moment;

a visit to Cabo might be just what he and Jojo needed before the baby was born. But before his daydream went any further, Jack looked more closely at the computer. The ad for Cabo hadn't been there prior to his FaceTime call; that seemed a little too coincidental. He frowned at the image of the white cruise ship in the turquoise blue water—it was as though his computer had been listening.

He shut the laptop. There were still a few hours before his eleven o'clock meeting with his father-in-law, the president of China, Wang Yang. He wasn't entirely sure what the meeting was about, but when the president of China requests to meet with you, you don't turn him down.

"I haven't been able to fall back asleep." Jojo's voice beckoned him from the bedroom. Jack stood up, stretched, and went to her, removing his clothes as he crawled back into bed.

"How about we just go back to bed for the rest of the day," he said as she wrapped her arms around him.

"I thought that's what Sundays were supposed to be for," she said. "But you're the one who's going to be leaving soon. Why are you meeting with my dad on a Sunday, anyway?"

"Well, I didn't feel like I was really in the position to specify the day or time."

"It's okay. I have a few things to do around the house today, anyway."

"Oh yeah?"

"Yeah, I have to set up those shelves that just got delivered and I want to replace the front doorknob and lock; I got a much nicer one. And that sliding glass door in the back, it's good quality but it wasn't installed correctly. It needs a few small adjustments and then it should work just fine."

Jack smiled. "That's quite a list. You know, if it were me, I'd just call someone to do it. And hey, you forgot something on that list."

"Did I?"

"My massage."

She pushed back from him enough so he could see the playful smile on her face. "Your massage? Let me get your phone so you can call someone to do it."

They both laughed as Jojo pushed the covers back and sat up. "Roll over," she said.

"You don't really need to massage me right now. I should be massaging *you*—not only are you pregnant, you've got a full day of house restoration projects ahead of you."

"That's why you'll be giving me my massage later, once all my projects are complete."

"Ah," Jack said, turning onto his stomach as Jojo straddled his back. He let his eyes close as his wife's fingers, made strong from her years of sculpting, pressed the knotted muscles along his shoulder blades, either side of spine. "Now that's a plan."